# E.B. COLIN

 Kelpies

Kelpies is an imprint of Floris Books
First published in 2013 by Floris Books

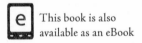 Published in partnership
with Strident Publishing

The publisher acknowledges subsidy from
Creative Scotland towards the publication
of this volume

This book is also
available as an eBook

British Library CIP data available
ISBN 978-178250-013-1
Printed in Poland

To the first three pyrates,
Theo, Frances and Oscar

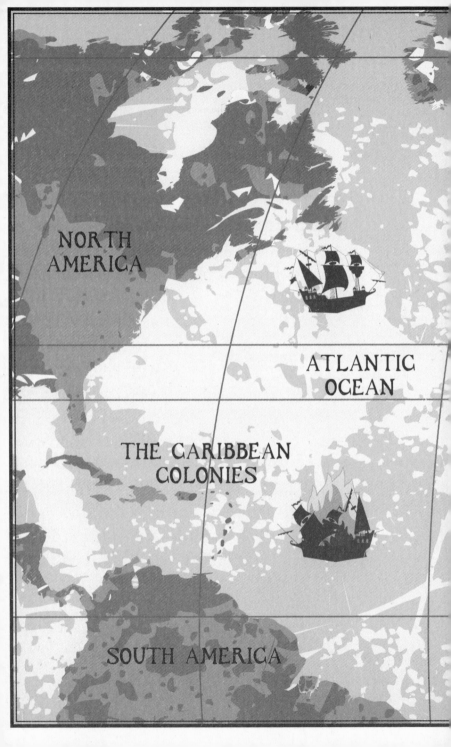

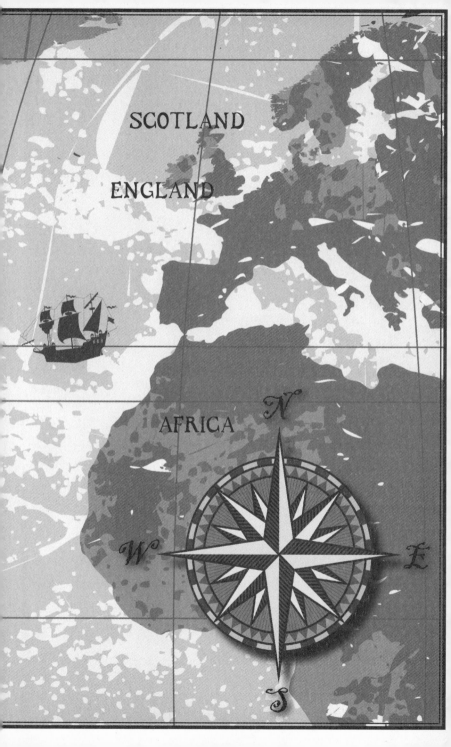

# THE CARIBBEAN COLONIES

CUBA

Kingston, Jamaica ✗

St Pierre, Martinique ✗

Caracas, Venezuela ✗

SOUTH AMERICA

BRITISH ISLES

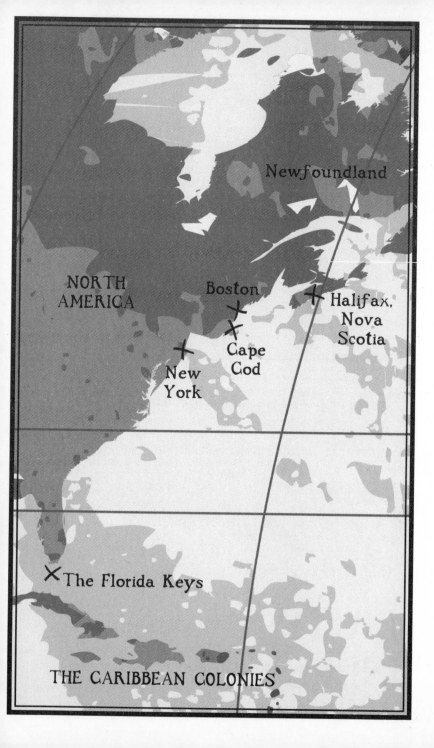

NORTH
AMERICA

Newfoundland

Boston

Halifax,
Nova
Scotia

New
York

Cape
Cod

The Florida Keys

THE CARIBBEAN COLONIES

# A BOX

It is as we are sailing away that I hear him. Not a voice, but the faintest of splashing. I look down and see the small bump of a nose and a swirl of hair just above the ocean's surface.

'There's someone in the water,' I shout. 'A boy!'

Our captain, Black Johnnie, looks down and sees him too.

'Heave to!' he yells. 'Man overboard!'

'He ain't one of ours,' says Bart, the navigator. 'Are you sure? Fast in, fast out, you always say.'

'We have enough time,' he replies and nods back at the *White Stag*, the Merchant Navy ship we have just plundered. 'Look how she blazes.'

The boat is on fire: the decks, the masts, even the

sails, are in flames. It fills the night with the roar of burning timber and the leap of orange and yellow.

Heading for Scotland, the *White Stag* had been loaded up with sugar and tobacco, with molasses and rum from the Colonies. We had spied her from afar and then crept up in her wake in the pale glimmer of dawn. Rather than resist, the crew had welcomed us on board and declared mutiny. McGregor was the name of their former captain. After the crew had restrained him, we had tied him up with rope along with two soldiers sent to guard the ship. And then we had thrown them into a small rowboat with enough bread and water to last a couple of days and cast them adrift.

We took the *White Stag's* cargo, plus six trunks full of silver and gold coins we found in the captain's cabin, loaded it in our hold, then gave the crew their promised cut, a chest of French doubloons to split. Once the crew were all aboard the ship's dinghy, they threw a lighted torch into the *White Stag's* hold.

'Good riddance,' one of them had shouted. 'May your timbers sink to the bottom of the sea and rot!'

'And as for you, Captain McGregor,' another yelled, 'may the sharks be more merciful than you ever were.'

It clearly hadn't been a happy voyage so far.

As we keel round to pick up the boy, however, a

musket fires. In the spill of light from the blazing cargo ship, the rowboat appears. McGregor and his soldiers have managed to escape the ropes and now, to our surprise, they seem to be pursuing us.

'Who tied the knots?' demands Black Johnnie.

'You did,' I tell him.

He frowns, then looks as if he is going to deny it. But this is no time for an argument.

'Just get the lad on board,' he shouts. 'As quick as you can.'

The boy looks about seven or eight years old and should weigh next to nothing. And yet it takes four men to drag him out of the water. We soon realise why. Padlocked around his ankle is a thick metal chain, which plummets right down to the seabed. If we want to save him, we have to pull up the chain. And whatever is at the end of it.

Another bullet whistles past us. The rowboat is coming closer. We don't fire back. Although none of us would admit it, the guns we use for raids are only for show. Right now we have about two bullets between us. We have cutlasses and dirk knives in our belts, but they are not much use at this distance.

And so we haul length after length of the chain over the side as fast as we can. But it is a very long chain. Bullets begin to whistle over our heads and we keep ducking to avoid them. Several hit our ship's bow and, like a tap turned on, a stream of seawater begins to pour into the hull.

'Is there more chain?' asks our captain.

There is more chain. Lots more. Our efforts are beginning to look increasingly futile. Sensing this, the boy begins to sob.

'You could cut off the foot,' someone offers, which only makes him cry harder.

'Not a good plan,' says Black Johnnie.

The same thought that has occurred to me must have occurred to him. Whatever is at the end of the chain is so valuable that the child has been made into a human buoy, whose body, dead or alive – as long as the fish don't get there first – will mark the spot.

'Work faster,' he tells the crew. 'All hands to it.'

The rowboat is so close now that I can hear the strain of effort of the men as they row. McGregor is standing in the bow, the musket in his hands aimed straight at Black Johnnie. Only the swell of the sea makes him hesitate. But as he comes nearer, the size of his target increases. Black Johnnie, however, hasn't noticed.

I open my mouth to shout out. But by the time I have my captain's attention it might already be too late. Since I'm eleven and not allowed to handle a gun, I raise my own weapon – a slingshot loaded with pebbles – and fire. I hit McGregor square in the jaw so hard that he staggers and falls back into the sea with a loud splash. The soldiers raise their oars and rush to help him. The whole boat starts to list to one side; clearly none of them has had much rowing experience. Even as I watch, however, McGregor clambers out of the water and over the side. He is younger and fitter than he looks. As soon as he is back in the boat he scans our crew and picks me out. His stare makes something inside me run cold. At first I think it is the gash on his forehead or the hiss and creak of the blazing cargo ship behind him as it starts to go down. And then I realise with a shiver what it is. I've seen his face before.

'How much more?' Black Johnnie shouts as the marines slice the oars back into the water and start to row. 'We must be almost there.'

'Got it!' shouts one of the men as the end of the chain falls with a clatter on to the deck. Attached to its end is an ordinary-looking box made of lead.

'Bring to.' Red Will at the bridge reacts immediately. 'Keep her full before the wind! Aloft!'

Our ship, the *Tenacity*, is a schooner. With its narrow hull and shallow draft, she is one of the fastest ships on the ocean. We turn, the sails fill up with wind, then we billow forward and begin to slip across the sea as smoothly as a swan. McGregor and the soldiers bob helplessly in our wake.

'Start rowing,' I yell back at them. 'If you're lucky you might reach dry land in a week.'

They do not look amused.

On deck, all attention turns to the boy. One seaman hurries below decks to find a gully knife to prise open his shackles, another to bring up a flagon of water or something stronger. But still he cowers beneath the bow looking terrified. It is not the fact that he almost drowned that frightens him. It is his present company: us.

'Are you pyrates?' he whispers.

'We are Gentlemen of Fortune,' I reply. 'Brave, proud and free.'

He closes his eyes, and seems to shrink – as if by sheer force of will he could make himself disappear.

I leave him alone, as this seems the only possible kindness, and find Black Johnnie standing on the bridge, a picture of elegance in his green velvet frockcoat and scarlet pantaloons. His hat is cocked and his boots shine like black glass. He gives a nod back to the rowboat. I can just about make out the furious faces of McGregor and the rowers, but we are moving swiftly away from them.

'Maybe we were a little harsh,' Black Johnnie says.

'In my opinion, that man deserves more than a pebble in the face,' I reply.

'So what would you advocate, Silas?'

'I myself would like him immersed in seawater for a considerable time to see how he likes it.'

Only in the middle of my words, I yawn. I can't help it; I have been up all night. Black Johnnie smiles down at me.

'Would you indeed?' he says softly.

I hear it before he does: the firing of a musket at the very end of its range. The shot hits him in the left shoulder, with such force that he is thrown back against the rail.

'Well, I'll be damned, he got me.' Black Johnnie sounds surprised rather than hurt. And even though he is a grown man, he closes his eyes and passes out.

## THE CAPTAIN'S REQUEST

'Captain's been hit!' I yell. 'Black Johnnie's been hit!'

When the crew realise what's happened, every one of them drops what they are doing and runs to the captain's side. The surgeon, who doubles as the cook, lets the salt-cod stew burn, the watch is abandoned, even the Jolly Roger flag, in the middle of being taken down by the fourth mate, flaps loose on its ropes and then blows away. Only our course, the wheel secured by a length of rope, doesn't waver.

'I'll survive,' says Black Johnnie when he comes round. 'But look at my beautiful coat. It's ruined!'

The velvet is soaked right through, now black instead of green.

'I'll fix it,' I tell him. 'Or maybe I won't. In my

opinion, the colour never did suit you.'

'Indeed?' says Black Johnnie. 'Thank you for that.'

Everyone laughs and I'm not sure quite why. I feel colour rise right to the roots of my hair.

'Will you do something else for me, Silas?' the captain asks as the surgeon works on his shoulder.

'Of course,' I reply, thinking he is going to ask me to fetch him something from below, a glass of fresh water or a clean rag.

'Take care of the boy,' he says. 'We don't want him dead before we can put him off in a safe place.'

'But what about the box?' I ask.

'Leave the box,' he says. 'Let him keep it until his guard has dropped. We don't want to frighten him any further.'

How can I say no? The captain's injury is, in a roundabout kind of way, my fault. If I hadn't spotted the boy in the sea then none of this would have happened.

I find the boy curled up and fast asleep in the same place I left him. He is pale and small and the skin around his right ankle is red and bruised. His feet are bare and turning blue with cold. It is a wonder, not just that he has survived his ordeal, but that he has survived a life at sea at all. He has something wrapped up in his arms: the lead box. In his sleep, he whimpers, and as I watch, he starts to weep.

'No,' he mutters in a dream. His voice is refined, Scottish, but not entirely so. 'You let me be!'

If he were awake, I would set him straight. I would tell him that he need not be scared. I would assure him that he will come to no harm. If he believes that pyrates are cowardly and cruel, lacking in basic morality and dressed in rags, then he has been fooled. Picaroons, buccaneers, Brethren of the Coast, are the most courageous, most generous, most colourful men that ever sailed.

He may have been told that the Golden Age of Pyracy is over. It is true that the days of Kidd and Blackbeard, Every, Tew and Low, when the seas were abob with precious things and the gallows were nothing more than an idle threat, are gone. With so many ships ploughing back and forth between Europe and the Americas, and so much easy wealth to be made, the trade routes are now closely patrolled. If caught, a pyrate can expect no sympathy. The sentence is death.

And yet, although we may be the last of our kind, I doubt that any of us would choose another life. Although our skins are black, white, brown, yellow and red, we dress like royalty in satin and silk and velvet. And no matter where we have come from, no matter what we have done or what has been done to us, we have sworn on our life to equality, to loyalty and freedom. How do I know? Because I was lost and then was saved and now I am a pyrate's boy.

I will do as Black Johnnie asks. I will watch over the boy with the box.

While I am looking at him, however, his eyes suddenly spring open and he sits up straight.

'It's locked,' he says. But his face says more: *if you touch the box, I shall jump back overboard.*

# A PASSAGE TO THE COLONIES

The sun is high in the sky and I am lying in the cool shade of my bunk. We are anchored in the bay of a small island, one in an archipelago of about twenty that is strung in a long, loose line, in the Caribbean Sea. This island, like the rest, is uninhabited and there are plenty of coves and bays and tiny inlets to hide a ship or two. Lush green forests rise up from the beach and the air smells of warm earth and fresh spice and ripe fruit.

The bullet in Black Johnnie's shoulder has been removed, the injury bandaged up. Even though it could have been much worse, he won't be able to use his left arm until the wound heals. Luckily he's right-handed. On days like these, he writes long letters with a quill pen and Indian ink that leaves dark stains on his lips and fingers. The crew say he sends them to a woman in Cape Cod, a woman whom he loves but whose wealthy family would never accept an outlaw like him. They laugh openly at the idea that he might take a good haul one day, settle down, turn respectable, then ask for her hand in marriage.

'Black Johnnie *respectable*!' they say. 'Now that's something I'd like to see.'

Right now I can hear whoops of their laughter as they dive off the deck into sea so blue and clear you'd want to take a drop of it to wear around your neck. Later, they'll sleep and eat, count up coins and calculate how much money we've made.

The boy we pulled out of the sea lies just across from me in the spare bunk. He has the lead box beneath him, even though it must feel like a brick. He is too young to sail on our ship for long – the pyrate code does not allow young children or women on board – but I am longing to know what happened to him and how he ended up in the sea chained to his precious box.

When I ask if he'd like to go up for a breath of air, he shakes his head: *no*. And when the men start to sing and joke and laugh and use rough language the way they always do when they've had a shot of grog mixed with the juice of a mango, he pulls the blanket right over his face.

I remember my first day aboard the pyrates' schooner. I was so scared by the sound of knives being sharpened and the smell of fish and coconuts that I wouldn't come out of my bunk. Gradually, however, I began to listen to the way the men talked to each other and hear them joke and tease and, although their table manners are appalling and many of them smell a bit, it wasn't long before I saw that they were nothing like I expected. I thought they would chop me up and eat me. Instead, they took me in and fed me when I was half-starved and dressed in rags. Then they gave me leather shoes and silk stockings and buckled breeches, and kept me. Being kept, to me at least, was a completely new experience.

My name is Silas Orr. I have been called many things in my life so far, not all of them complimentary. Just like my sister, Agnes, who is older by four years, I have pale blue eyes, brown hair and the kind of skin that freckles as soon as the sun comes out.

We were born in the town of Greenock on the west coast of Scotland. I remember the wind on the silver-grey surface of the river Clyde, the shipping lanes filled with the white sails of ships and fishing boats, and the mountains that rose up beyond, purple in summer and capped in snow all winter. It was where my mother had come from, those mountains, although I never really met her. She left this earth just two hours after I was born. My father was a church minister and when I was six, he sent me to the parish school with Agnes to learn to read and write. A year later, there was an outbreak of fever in the town and he too died. The church congregation, with every good intention, stepped in to organise for our needs. I was adopted by a brewer and his wife, and Agnes was sent to Glasgow to work as a housemaid.

The brewer and his wife had no children but claimed they treated me like their own anyway. This meant working six days a week, regular beatings and lectures on sin. Every now and then on a Sunday my sister would travel back to see me. She always brought me a gift: an apple or a lemon. After a few years, the bloom was gone from her cheeks, her face was white and her dress worn thin at the knees from scrubbing floors. I was sitting on the quay with her in the cold, grey rain one Sunday, watching the ships sail by and trying to guess which were heading to the Americas.

'That one,' she said with certainty, pointing to a schooner with a wide prow and many sails unfurled on its three masts. 'You can almost smell the sunshine.'

And then she sighed.

'What's the matter?' I asked.

'How I wish I had another life,' she said.

As the rain came down and the ship sailed away, I made a decision. I would set out to seek my fortune, to make a new life for both of us. The very next day I ran away from the brewer and headed to Port Glasgow where a ship was just about to sail for Jamaica. Along with one other boy and a girl a year older than me, I signed a bond and agreed to work for seven years in exchange for the price of my fare.

'Who is your guarantor?' the bondsman asked.

'What's that?' I asked.

He sighed and explained it was the person who would be asked to pay for my return fare if anything went amiss. I told him that this wouldn't happen.

'Name?' he insisted. 'There must be someone!'

'Agnes Orr,' I said because she was the only person I had.

He wrote her name and address in a large ledger.

I had no idea what a nightmare the voyage would be, but at least it took my mind off the terrible sadness of leaving my sister. We sailed in January on a journey that took almost three months. The ship was small, inhabited by more rats than crew and passengers, and it leaked. The area where we slept sloshed with water for most of the journey. Twice a day, we were given wheat biscuits filled with weevils, and watered-down rum. The other boy refused to eat or drink anything. One morning he simply disappeared. I never found out what had happened but the girl, Catherine, said he had probably died during the night and his body had been tipped over the side before any other passengers woke.

'How will his family know what happened to him?' I asked.

'A sea captain has the authority to do all sorts of things,' she told me. 'To marry people; to record births and deaths. One of the crew told me he's written our death certificates out already, just in case.'

'That's horrible,' I said.

So I forced myself to eat and drink whatever I was given, no matter that it still crawled within my mouth or burned down my throat like fire.

Some days we talked about where we had come from and where we were going. Catherine told me she had run away from a cruel aunt (she didn't mention parents), who was planning to marry her off to an elderly neighbour when she reached the age of twelve.

'I would not do it,' she said simply. 'Not for all the tea in China.'

I told her of my plan – how once I had paid off my

bond, I would settle in the Colonies, make my fortune, then send for Agnes.

'I wish I had a brother like you,' Catherine said.

She looked at me and I felt a warm glow in my chest. When the wind raged and our bellies ached with hunger, when we feared that the boat would sink or capsize or crash into rocks, when I was sick and could barely raise my head over a bucket, she never stopped telling me that we were almost there.

'We will get to the Colonies,' she whispered. 'And in seven years' time we will be free.'

We finally reached our destination, Kingston on the island of Jamaica, one windy day in March. As she was handed over to a woman with a sour expression, Catherine turned and I saw doubt cross her face for the first time.

'We'll see each other again, won't we, Silas?'

'Of course,' I replied. 'I'll come and find you. When I have a day off.'

'Not if I find you first,' she smiled.

I had no idea then that finding each other would be impossible. Catherine and I were not going to be leading visiting kinds of lives. My new master, a man called Ferguson, owned a sugar plantation in Orange Bay. He lived in a huge white house with a wide wooden porch that I was not allowed to enter. This was one of many rules. I was forbidden to eat the fruit in the orchard and I was forbidden to leave the plantation under any circumstance. At night the door to my room was locked. If I was caught breaking any rule, my bond would be revoked and I would be sent back to where I came from on the first available ship at Agnes's – my guarantor's – expense.

I had been hired to work in the gardens. Even though there was jungle all around, Ferguson's garden had been laid out with lawns and flowerbeds in the English style. The gardens had to be neatly trimmed and kept free of weeds. It was so hot and damp, however, that while native plants grew almost before your eyes, the flowers and shrubs that Ferguson imported from Europe wilted or died. My job was to hack down some and nurture others. Sometimes I got the two confused and was caned for it.

Although it seemed a never-ending job, it was not hard work, not compared to working in the sugar-cane fields or in the grinding and boiling houses. This was done by black slaves. I'd never seen a black man before I arrived in Jamaica and the first time I saw one, I stopped and gawped. His skin was dark, darker even than the church pews back at home. He handed me a hunk of raw sugar cane. I didn't know what to do with it and so he hacked another piece, held it to his mouth and sucked. I did the same and my mouth was filled with the sweetest syrup I had ever tasted.

'Good?' he asked.

'Aye,' I replied.

In time, I got used to the heat and the humidity, I learned which plant was precious and which was a weed, and began to cut my own raw sugar cane straight from the field. I wrote once to Agnes, just to say I was well. I imagined a bright future for me and for her, as Jamaica was indeed the land of opportunity. Once I was old enough and had paid off my bond, there were plenty of positions on the plantations for a Scot with a head for figures and a grasp of letters. I was sure that seven years would pass before I knew it.

Then one day, about a year after I started working in Ferguson's garden, a lady arrived from Scotland unexpectedly. I was wanted back urgently, she said. She wouldn't say why or by whom but only that all would be explained in due course. My bond was to be repaid, plus a little extra, and I was to be taken to Glasgow on the next sailing from Kingston.

# KINGSTON TOWN

My elation at the prospect of seeing my sister again was swiftly followed by a worry. What of my plans? What of my new life? I was going back to where I started from with nothing to show for it. And who could possibly want me and why? I was at a loss.

A ship was soon due to dock at Kingston. It was to be loaded with goods before heading back to Scotland. The lady who had been hired to accompany me home was sweaty and flustered. She had come to Jamaica to visit relatives but had found the bright colours, pungent smells and hot sun of the tropics too much to bear. She looked at the world, me included, with obvious distaste.

'Will he be shackled?' she asked Ferguson.

I looked at the door and briefly considered running

through it and taking my chances in the jungle. Three months at sea in chains? Whatever awaited me in Glasgow must indeed be bad.

The plantation owner shook his head.

'I don't think it will be necessary,' he said. 'Give me a minute with the boy.'

Ferguson took me aside and leant down low to speak. 'The paperwork is all complete, but it is dependent upon your safe arrival in Glasgow. If this lady reports that you've run off, your guarantor will be left to foot the bill of your journey. Do you understand?'

I nodded my head.

'Don't look so worried,' he said. 'This lady has been paid good money to bring you back. You must be worth a penny or two to someone.'

'Well?' the lady said.

'He won't bolt,' the plantation owner told her.

'As long as you're sure,' she said. 'Anyway, my fee was paid in advance.'

In my room, I packed up a few mementos – a perfect shell I had found on the beach, a feather from a brightly coloured bird and a slingshot I had made myself, along with a small bag of pebbles – and climbed up beside the driver of the pony and trap that would take us to Kingston.

The lady spent the whole journey clutching her bag and complaining about everything: the Blue Mountains, the slaves in the fields and the lush green forests. Even the villages, called after Scottish towns such as Glasgow and Campbeltown, offended her. Worse than that, she had an attack of the wind, as she called it, and made the sweet Jamaican air stink.

We had left the plantation at daybreak and it was just after four in the afternoon when we drove into town. She booked herself into a hotel and told the keeper to lay out some straw for me in the stables. Then she gave me some change for bread and told me to go away and not disturb her until the morning.

I wandered through the town, spent a few pennies at a market stall on cassava cakes and fried yams and savoured each mouthful. Soon, I told myself, all I would eat would be porridge and herring.

In Kingston, every second accent was Scottish. But there were also Chinamen, Dutchmen, Spaniards, Portuguese and a few Englishmen. I walked along the harbour and gazed out at the schooners and galleons and warships that were anchored and wondered where they had come from. On the other side of the water I noticed the ruins of a town, half sunk into the sea. I asked a longshoreman what it was called.

'That's Port Royal,' he said. 'And that there's Gallows Point.'

He told me that until quite recently it had been the capital of Jamaica. Built on a spit of land and ringed with forts, the town was known all over the Colonies as a place where pyrates and fortune hunters came to spend their ill-gotten gains. It had more taverns, expensive shops and luxurious villas than anywhere else on the globe.

'It was rightly known as a den of iniquity,' the longshoreman said. 'Know what that is?'

I shook my head.

'Good lad,' he said. 'The longer you are ignorant of such places the better.'

Thirty years ago, Port Royal had been hit by an earthquake and a tidal wave. The whole town collapsed or sank, and thousands of people died. Since then, he told me, it was said to be cursed. Every time anyone tried to rebuild it, it was hit by hurricanes or burnt down by fire. In recent years it had been used for only one thing. Captured pyrates were taken there to an army garrison called Fort George.

'And then they get what they deserve,' he said.

'What would that be?' I asked.

'They swing from the gallows, of course,'

He held out a wavering finger towards the ruined town.

'Right there. But there are always more of them, filthy rotten pyrates who'd slit your throat as soon as look at you. See this?'

He turned his face to the side and I saw the white line of a scar running from his ear to his mouth.

'And I was one of the lucky ones,' he said.

A blood red sun was setting behind Port Royal. I looked out across the water and thought I saw the limp shape of a body, hanging. I ran back into the town as fast as I could and didn't stop until I reached the inn. But that night I slept badly. My dreams were full of blood-curdling cries and raised cutlasses: of pyrates. Also, just as I suspected, the straw was infested. When I woke up in the morning, my body was covered in tiny red bites.

# THE SHIP OF MISERY

The lady from Scotland seemed in a better mood and ordered me a breakfast of rice and peas. When I thanked her, she admitted that whoever had sent for me had provided six doubloons that I could use 'for my expenses'.

'Not that you'll find much to spend it on in this Godforsaken place,' she said as she handed me the coins, less the price of my breakfast. It was more money than I had ever seen before, not to say held in my own hand. I tied the coins up in a cloth purse and wore it round my neck.

Our ship, the lady said, was due to dock that morning. We sat in the waiting room of the shipping company down by the harbour. At lunchtime, when the sun was highest, our boat still hadn't docked. My travelling companion was asleep with her mouth open. I wandered along the dock and noticed a boat that hadn't been there the night before. It sat low in the water and looked even worse than the ship I had arrived on. But it was the sound that caught my attention, a sound so low that I only caught it when the wind was blowing in the right direction – the sound of moaning, one of the most awful things I had ever heard.

I had to see who or what was on board. I waited until the crew had all headed into a tavern and then, as silently as I could, I crept up the gangway. The first thing that hit me was the smell, an indescribable smell of despair and filth, rottenness and dead things. I lifted the hatch to the hold. A single shaft of light illuminated a sight I will never forget. Chained by their ankles and wrists, so close to each other that they could barely move, were dozens of African men, women and children. Their lips were swollen and their skin had a grey pallor that I hadn't seen on the slaves on the plantation. Had they travelled across an ocean like this? By their wasted bodies and dulled eyes, it was clear that they had. One of them, a man with a scar, looked at me and mouthed a word: *water*.

With my heart racing and tears in my eyes, I ran down the gangplank to the waiting room where a jar of fresh water had been left for the passengers.

You see, although I had never seen a black person before I arrived in Jamaica, I, too, had been bound to a plantation owner. And now I was angry, I was outraged, I was heartbroken. No living being deserved to be packed on board a boat like a piece of cargo.

The jar was heavy and I tried not to spill it as I hurried back up the gangplank. The African with the scar looked up at me. A drop of water fell on his face and he closed his eyes in anticipation. But how was I going to get it to him? How could he drink? His hands were chained together and I didn't have a cup. From the shore came the rough shouts of farewell from the tavern. The crew were coming back.

Without a second's hesitation, I emptied the jar into the hold over the Africans' parched faces and chests. And then I quickly lifted the hatch and shifted it back into place. I took one final glance down. The slave with the scar was staring up at me, his eyes blinking with thanks. And I felt ashamed, ashamed that I had done so little.

Later, I watched as the slaves were unloaded and herded into the merchant's yard. Almost as many dead bodies were brought off the ship as living ones. Those who had survived were in a terrible state: naked, half-starved and frightened.

It was then that I spotted the man who had crammed

so many people into his ship. Small, with thinning hair, he had a mouth that curled down most unattractively. When the man with the scar walked past him, he suddenly lashed out.

'What did you say?' he roared at the man.

'They speak no English, Captain McGregor,' his first mate declared.

'Hold him down,' shouted the man.

I could see only the backs of the four men restraining the man with the scar, but later I learned what had happened. McGregor had cut out the man's tongue with a knife. I could not have imagined a more horrible deed.

For what seemed like forever, the Africans stood in pens under the burning sun, like cattle. Many of them fainted in the heat and were poked until they stood up again. Finally the buyers arrived, plantation owners and slave dealers who had come to buy new slaves to take to the tobacco fields of Chesapeake or the sugar-cane fields of Barbados or Guadeloupe. They began to assemble behind a barrier. When it was raised, they rushed forward and began to grab the slaves they wanted, pulling mothers away from their children and men from their wives. The Africans reacted with shock. As one, they began to move back, back towards the dock and away from the slave dealers and plantation owners. Several men broke through the barrier and began to run. The first mate ran after them with a stick. But he did not seem too concerned. The only place they could go was the sea. Two were caught but not the third. On the edge of the dock the third man hesitated and looked back. It was the African with the scar who had just had his tongue cut out. The first mate raised his stick. The man jumped.

'It's all right,' the first mate shouted. 'They don't swim.'

But this man did. He swam and kept on swimming towards the open sea until the tiny black dot that was his head got smaller and smaller and finally disappeared.

'Well, I'll be damned,' the first mate said.

I like to hope that the water I threw over him gave him the strength he needed to escape. But it was not enough to shift the shame I felt when I saw how the slaves who remained were treated.

# THE VOYAGE

Later that afternoon, our ship arrived. It was quickly loaded up with tobacco and sacks of sugar and molasses all bound for a refinery in Greenock.

'Hallelujah,' the lady said as we boarded.

But I turned my back and wept as we sailed out of Kingston, and I didn't care who saw it. My life had been laid out in front of me with six years left before I would be free, before I could establish myself and send for my sister, before I might find Catherine again. I would never see her now. And I could not offer Agnes a new life. Everything I had planned had come to nothing. I had no idea what would become of me.

For five days the journey was uneventful. The wooden hull of our ship creaked as it ploughed through the ocean, and the sails snapped on their ropes as the wind lulled and then rallied up again. I found a spot by the bowsprit where I could lie low, invisible to everyone, and spent my days watching out for the plume of a whale or the leap of a dolphin. But I saw nothing, nothing but the occasional herring gull that would cruise above and stare down at me with a single, yellow eye.

On the sixth day the sky up ahead turned dark. While a low sun lit up the sails with a pale yellow light, storm clouds billowed purple, black and grey. A chill wind came first, which left the taste of metal in my mouth. And then the sea began to heave, the swell growing bigger and bigger. It was as if the playful waves of coastal waters had been replaced by eyeless monsters who rolled and hauled clumsily around us. The rain fell first in huge drops, then hurled down as hail in freezing arrows of ice. The wind blew hard, then harder still and great waves began to crash down on our decks. It seemed as if we were already underwater, toiling forward against the current but driven back again and again.

The captain ordered that the cargo be jettisoned. Sacks of sugar were heaved overboard and immediately sank without trace. Next were barrels of molasses and six hogsheads of tobacco. Any luggage belonging to passengers was also dumped over the side – the lady who had been sent to fetch me wept as she watched her trunk slip beneath the surface – but still we took in more water than it was possible to bale out. Eventually it was clear that we were not sailing any more, but sinking.

'Man the cockboat,' shouted the captain. 'Abandon ship.'

There were more than fifty of us on board and one small dinghy. There wasn't room for more than a dozen. The lady, being the only woman, was helped into a place.

'I'll say he drowned in the storm,' she said to the other passengers. 'It was not my fault. Thankfully I was paid in advance.'

'Who sent for me?' I shouted above the wind. 'Tell me their name!'

I thought she had not heard me, or was pretending she hadn't. But then, with an almighty jerk, the cockboat suddenly dropped a few feet as the seamen loosened the ropes, and she yelled out, 'Crawlfish and swim!'

This made no sense, no sense at all, so I begged her to repeat it.

'Crawford and Swann!' she yelled again.

The boat fell a few feet further and hit the water with an almighty splash. The names still meant nothing to me. I called out once more but my voice was lost in the roar of the wind.

With six seamen manning the oars, the rowboat began to pull off, rising up, over, and finally disappearing behind the crest of a huge black wave. Nobody ever saw it again.

# THE RESCUE

The sinking ship groaned as it listed steeply to the left. Without a full crew to man it, the sails ripped and the masts – the main, the fore and the mizzen – snapped one by one. Those of us left behind began to grab anything we could find that would float: doors were ripped from their hinges and hatches lifted from the hold, caskets kicked apart and barrels emptied. And then the others wished each other luck and launched themselves over the side. I hesitated. I had been taught how to read and write but not how to swim. The decks pitched suddenly and the force threw me overboard. Even now I shudder as I recall the way the sea closed over my head and filled my mouth with the taste of salt. And then I remember nothing.

I don't know why I didn't drown, dragged down by the ship as it sank to the bottom of the sea. But when I woke up hours later, I was lying on top of one side of a wooden packing crate with the name

## FELIX PARSONS

painted on it. I still have no idea who Felix Parsons was and what it was he had paid to have shipped back from Jamaica, but in the night and day that followed I began to think of him a friend. I talked to him when I was cold and lonely and scared that I would drown. And he kept me afloat, quite literally.

Although I tried not to think of it, I knew that with no fresh water, out on the open sea, I couldn't last for more than a couple of days. I scanned the horizon back and forth, looking hard for any ships or signs of land.

Night was falling on my second day adrift when I spotted a ship.

I waved and shouted and would have leapt for joy if I had been able.

Although I was thirsty and burned by the sun, I

knew I would survive. Once I had been rescued, I would ask to be taken back to Jamaica. My life could resume. But as the ship came closer I realised that I had rejoiced too soon. This was no merchant ship. I ripped a length of wood from the edge of the packing crate, exposing a nail and making my raft much smaller. I needed something to defend myself with. The flag the ship flew was black – a Jolly Roger.

As the hull approached I prepared for a fight. Who knew what they would do to me? Make me walk the plank? Dance barefoot on sharpened swords? Anything was possible – these men were pyrates!

A black face looked down at me, a familiar black face. I lowered my weapon. It was the slave who had swum away from the dock at Kingston. Another face appeared behind his, a man's face with kind eyes and a lopsided smile.

'Good evening,' he said. 'You look as if you're a long way from home.'

A line was thrown and, after a moment's hesitation, I grabbed it and tied it around my waist. Stepping off the raft, and much to the amusement of the crew, I turned upside down and was dragged, half underwater, half on the surface, towards the ship. The captain reached down, took my foot, and with one swift yank, pulled me onboard.

That day Black Johnnie was wearing a scarlet silk shirt, blue velvet breeches and a black frockcoat trimmed with gold embroidery. His shoes were polished and fastened with silver buckles, and he wore his black hair long and tied at the nape of his neck with a ribbon. Apart from the musket in his belt, he would not have looked out of place in a king's palace. He glanced down at my tattered clothes but didn't say anything. Instead he asked me where I had come from and where I was heading. And then he bowed when I explained what had happened, and he told me I was a lucky blighter.

After I had undressed, washed in a bucket of clean water and eaten a plate of fresh fruit and biscuits, I wrapped myself in a blanket, lay down on a bunk I had been given in the depths of the stern and closed my eyes. But I could not sleep. Although I was exhausted, I was convinced that the pyrates might creep in and grab me when I wasn't expecting it. And so I lay in the dark and listened to their voices on deck. They were arguing. I supposed they were debating whether to kill me now and cook me or keep me for another day. My fear overwhelmed my exhaustion. You see, since my father had died, I had rarely been shown kindness and simply didn't recognise it any more. I got up and dressed quickly.

I guessed by the sticky heat and the cry of the gulls

that we couldn't be too far from land. Perhaps the currents would wash me to shore, or at least take me as far from the pyrates as possible. And so, as quietly as I could, I crept up the wooden ladders to the decks. At the far end a small fire was burning on a box of sand and the air smelled of roasting banana. The pyrates sitting around the fire broke into song.

I admit that the sea looked blacker and deeper than I remembered. I no longer had Felix Parsons so I quickly untied a small rowboat that was stowed above the gun deck, managed to hoist it out over the side and then lowered it down so gently that it landed in the sea with only the smallest of splashes. I climbed over the wooden railings. It was not far to jump. All I had to do was launch myself forward.

A hand landed gently on my shoulder. I swung round with both fists raised. It was the black slave. He looked at me with wide eyes. What was I doing, he seemed to ask?

'I have to go,' I said. 'You can come with me, if you want?'

He didn't answer but turned. And right there was the pyrate captain, his eyes black in the flickering light of the fire. He glanced over the side to where the rowboat was bobbing.

'You're leaving us?' he asked.

I didn't answer. It was quite obvious what I was going to do.

'What's this?' he said and, reaching out, appeared to take something from behind my ear. He opened his hand to reveal a small silver compass.

'I didn't take it,' I said, in case he thought I was a thief.

He placed it in my hand.

'If you head west, within two days you should reach Chesapeake,' he told me. 'But try and avoid *La Vibora*, that's 'the viper' in Spanish, a big bank of reef and sand shaped like a snake. Treacherous, unfortunately. Can't see the dangers until it's too late. Many a ship has gone down there. Anyway, good luck.'

He stood back. He was going to let me go. And yet my boat had already begun to float away.

'And then again, it might be better to leave at first light,' the captain suggested. His voice was rich and deep. He was Scottish, that much I could tell but I wondered where he had grown up. Not in Greenock, for sure. 'Unless you know the stars,' he went on, 'or the moon is full, you might find it easier to navigate by day.'

For a moment or two we stared out at the sea. The boat, by now, was gone.

'Anyway,' said the captain turning to me again. 'We were discussing your arrival earlier. We had a vote. You see, we don't allow children on the ship. Or women, but —'

'I'm not a child,' I replied. 'I am eleven years old.'

'Please,' he said quietly. 'Don't interrupt. It was decided that on this occasion, and since you had someone to vouch for you —' he nodded towards the African man, 'Toombi here — it was decided that we would offer you a position on board, if, of course, you decide against trying your luck on the open sea.'

I was so taken aback that my mouth fell open. The captain reached forward and with a single finger under my chin, he closed it.

'You will only have half the cut of the men, you will have to swear an oath to adhere to the pyrate code, and you will initially be on trial,' he said. 'But I think, with a bit of work, you might have the makings of a cabin boy.'

I looked him straight in the eye. 'I will not kill or maim,' I said.

'That is not quite what I had in mind,' the captain replied.

'Oh.' I pulled myself up to my full height. 'Just what will the position involve?' I asked.

Here, he looked a little embarrassed. 'Well,' he said. 'I like a shiny shoe and a clean shirt and there is so little time, so little time for that kind of toil. I thought that while you learn to be a seaman – although you seem to have acquired many skills already – you might also do that. For me.'

He cleared his throat and raised an eyebrow and then folded his arms. And then I looked at Toombi, the African who had escaped from the slave traders. No matter what had happened to him, he had vouched for me. Something within my chest cracked open. I glanced out at the sea. It had never looked particularly inviting. I was suddenly so tired that I couldn't help yawning. The captain slapped me gently on the shoulder.

'Why not sleep on it?' he suggested. 'You can tell me your answer in the morning. And you can keep the compass. You never know when it might come in useful.'

I woke up many hours later. Sunlight was streaming into the hold. Someone up above was singing an Irish jig. A plate of fresh mango had been laid out beside me for my breakfast. And then I knew. My answer was yes: ten, twenty, thirty times yes. Of course there have been hard times and lean times and times where I thought we were all going to die. But despite this, I have never for one moment regretted my decision.

The captain seemed pleased. He smiled and introduced himself as Jon Harkin. It is one of the few times I have ever heard him use his real name. Everyone called him Black Johnnie.

Sometimes I wonder what would have happened if I had slipped away faster, if I hadn't hesitated before hurling myself after the rowboat. And I see myself all alone in the middle of the ocean, floating endlessly, desperately scanning the horizon for any sign of dry land. I may have made it all the way to the American coast. But more likely I would not have.

And yet sometimes my freedom weighs heavily. While I am free, my sister, Agnes still toils like a slave. One day, I vow, I will save her, as I was saved. But when? And how? I have no idea, no idea at all. And so I push the idea down, deep down, where it hangs quiet but leaden inside me like a locked box on the end of a long chain.

# LIFE ON BOARD

In my dreams I hear my name spoken once, twice, three times. I only closed my eyes for a moment while I was keeping watch over the boy with the lead box, but must have fallen asleep. I sit up with a start. He is standing above me.

'Silas?' he says. 'Is that your name?'

'It is,' I say. 'What's yours?'

He glances over his shoulder before he speaks in case anyone should overhear.

'My mother called me James, but on the ship I got called Jimmy.'

His accent is Scottish.

'So what shall it be?' I ask.

'James, if you please,' he replies. And then he smiles,

the smallest of smiles.

'So, what is your story?' I ask.

But just then, from the deck just above our porthole, there is a scream followed by a loud splash. The boy cowers and climbs back into his bunk until all I can see is the flash of his eyes beneath the blanket.

He is too young to sail on our ship for long – the pyrate code does not allow it – but I would like to know what happened to him and how he ended up in the sea chained to his precious box. Even though it isn't legal, boys of his age are sometimes used as powder monkeys by the British Navy. They are small enough to run back and forth below decks bringing gunpowder to the cannons and cheap to feed on scraps. A year at sea with an average number of cannon firings, however, is enough to make most of them stone deaf. By the time they reach my age, their backs are curved from bending in small spaces and their growth is stunted.

But this boy was on a merchant ship, McGregor's ship. He is weak, but not deaf or curved. He sounds properly schooled. He cannot have been one of the crew. Was he a stowaway? But why would a boy with any other choice take on the hardships of a life at sea?

He hears me when I ask if he'd like to go up for a

breath of air but does not answer. The men are loud and merry, having had much rum and, hearing the carousing, he begins to sob again.

'It's only the men having fun,' I say. 'What do you think of the ship?'

He doesn't answer but I keep on talking anyway and gradually his sobbing subsides.

'This is the most beautiful ship in the world,' I tell him. 'Of all the ships I have sailed on – admittedly there have not been many – this ship is by far the best. Her name is *Tenacity*. That means toughness or persistence. I sometimes say it over and over just because I like the sound of it in my mouth.'

He is listening now. I can tell. And so I continue. I tell him that the ship was built in Jamaica as a gift for a sugar merchant's wife and was won by our captain three years ago in a card game. It has two masts, at the fore and the aft, and is armed with six guns. As well as Black Johnnie, the crew includes a navigator, a first mate, a surgeon and cook. Although there is not much room for supplies – it was designed to sail along coasts rather than across oceans – it is big enough for us.

'Once we get going,' I say, 'we slip over the surface of the sea like a skimming stone. Just look, look around you.'

He sits up and for the first time, he looks, really looks. The doors to the cabins are wreathed with holly leaves and the beams above our berths are decorated with images of mermaids. One of the carpenters who built her was an artist and you can see his hand in almost every single space on the ship; there are tiny mice carved into the table legs and bunches of grapes along the balustrades. But his finest achievement is the figurehead. Leading our way, positioned at the very tip of the prow, is a woman with red lips, an ample bosom and hair that sweeps down from her head in a cascade of painted gold curls.

'Her name,' I tell the boy, 'is Isabella.'

'That's my mother's name!' he replies.

'Is she pretty?' I ask.

'Very,' he replies.

He runs his fingers over a carving of a fish on the beam above his head.

'I hadn't noticed,' he said. 'Can I carve something?'

'Of course,' I say.

Like the skin of the pyrates, who are all covered in tattoos, our ship is a work in progress. The men have added new carvings of their own: dolphins, birds and sumptuous ladies. The names of their sweethearts are picked out on the mast and the places where they were born are carved on the hatches. Like sailors' tattoos that record full names and places of birth to identify their bodies in case of drowning, the *Tenacity* identifies the crew and their imaginings on its polished wood. To lose it would mean losing part of ourselves.

The morning air is hot and close and the sun falls in bright splashes on the floor. I have already spent hours polishing boots and stitching buttons, washing socks and swabbing the decks. So I lean back on my bunk, stretch out and close my eyes. We are safe here, safe at anchor in the most beautiful bay in the whole world, which is not only full of crabs and bluefish, but also hides us from any other ship that may happen to pass by.

Black Johnnie intends to sail to St Pierre on the French island of Martinique on the next tide. Britain and France are at war in America and no British naval ship would dare to follow us there. I have heard all about St Pierre. The town sits in the shadow of a volcano, and is full of beautiful women, French perfumers and tailors who can make anything you want in the space of a day. And so, after selling our latest haul to an acquaintance of the captain's, we will be free to wander the streets and spend our cut of the money in any way we wish. I can hardly wait.

'They'll come looking for the box,' the boy whispers, so softly that I barely hear him.

I open my eyes. He is still lying in his bunk but his face has clouded over with worry.

'What did you say?'

'They won't let it go.'

I sit up and look at him. Now he's holding the lead box in both hands.

'What's inside?' I ask.

He shakes his head and takes a step back.

'Let me take a look,' I say, and step towards him. But the boy opens his mouth and lets out a short high-pitched scream. His voice is surprisingly loud, considering the size of him.

Toombi appears at the door; he looks at me and then looks at the boy clutching the lead box, shakes his head and then starts to laugh. But, suddenly he holds a finger to his lips and cocks his head. In the distance is another sound, a sound we all recognise, a sound we all dread: the boom and whistle of a cannon being fired. With an explosive splash, a cannonball lands in the sea about twenty yards to the right of us.

'Told you so,' the boy says.

# THE NARROWS

Up on the deck, it is chaos. Everyone is arguing over what we should do. Man the cannons and fire back, some of the men suggest. Abandon ship. Scupper the *Tenacity*, make for the shore, hide out on the island and then pull her up again when they've gone. Black Johnnie, however, seems to have other plans. First he insists on absolute quiet. And then he sends me up to the crow's nest to take a look around. I shimmy up the rigging and climb the mainmast. Here the sway of the ship can be so strong that unless you have your wits about you, you are at risk of being flung out of the nest and into the sea.

Black Johnnie waves his hand at me to tell me to make it quick. I strain on my tiptoes, shade my eyes with my hand and peer into the distance. But I can't see the other ship over the bluff of land that separates us, no matter how high I stretch. I look down and shake my head. And then we all hear that dreadful noise again: the low boom of a firing and the whistle of another cannonball flying through the air. This time it lands ten feet to the left of us, throwing up a huge arc of water that splashes over the decks and sets our ship rocking back and forth. I hold on as tightly as I can and am flipped violently from side to side, wondering why on earth he sent me up here.

'Well?' asks the captain when I have my feet on the deck again. 'What did you see?'

'Nothing,' I tell them. 'I couldn't see anything.'

The pyrates start to panic, saying that our attacker has special seeing powers and that he will not stop firing until he hits us. Black Johnnie, however, simply climbs into a hammock that hangs from the rigging and closes his eyes.

'Captain,' they all start to whisper frantically, 'this is no time for a nap. What do we do? Tell us!'

'Do? We do nothing,' he says softly. 'If we can't see them then they can't see us. They're guessing; they're trying to provoke us into retaliation. You see, they might have a fair idea that we're hiding in the archipelago but, apart from the boy's scream, they have no idea exactly where. So follow my example, lie low and take a snooze, quietly of course.'

As if to back him up, we hear the blast of another cannon. The ball lands one hundred yards away on the far end of the bluff, felling several small trees and sending a clutch of indignant parakeets up into the air.

'What did I tell you?' The captain pulls his hat over his eyes. 'That ship is moving eastward. They won't trouble us now.'

But before there is even the chance to settle down, like Black Johnnie, and make ourselves comfortable, a blood-curdling scream comes from below, so loud and piercing that it must be audible from here to Kingston. The captain leaps out of the hammock.

'I said silence,' he says. 'Who is making that infernal racket?' There is no need to answer his question. We all know that it is the boy again. I reach him first. He is standing at the bottom of the stairs, his mouth open and that dreadful noise coming out.

'Stop,' I yell. But he won't. I put my hand across his mouth but he tries to bite me. He keeps screaming.

'What is it?' I shout. 'Tell me.'

But he is hysterical. His hands, I notice, are empty. He's lost the box.

'Who took his box?' Black Johnnie demands. 'Own up now, you scoundrels, and no one will be punished!'

Everyone looks at each other and in turn we shake our heads. We all look guilty, even me, and I know I haven't taken it. The whole boat shakes as a cannon ball lands only a few feet away. Whoever is firing has heard the boy's screams. Black Johnnie sighs and wipes his brow with his shirt.

'This demands a change of plan. All hands on deck,' he commands. 'We sail for Martinique immediately!'

The sails are rapidly unfurled and secured, and then we tack towards the mouth of the bay. As soon we reach the headland, a swell of wind takes us out into the open sea. At last we have a clear view of our pursuers and they of us. For a moment no one says a word. It a huge warship, a sixty-gunner, that carries about four hundred men. Nobody had been expecting anything like this. Sixty-gunners usually sail at the head of the British naval fleet to intimidate the enemy. McGregor must have given them the tip-off. They haven't come looking for the *box* but for *pyrates*!

There is a moment when nothing happens. The warship seems slow to react. Maybe they weren't expecting that we would come out of our hiding place and confront them.

'What are we going to do now?' I ask.

Black Johnnie looks at me as if I am slow.

'What do you think we're going to do,' he asks. 'Run away, of course.'

And then, just as a whistle blows on board the warship, the captain raises his arm.

'Make for the channel!' he shouts. The first mate spins the wheel and we veer off along the line of the coast.

I see now that our captain's plan is our only chance. Although warships like this one are virtually unsinkable and can withstand the kind of storms and heavy seas that would scupper most boats, they are also cumbersome and ride low in the water.

Our island is separated from its neighbour by a narrow strait. Here, the ocean is not more than six fathoms deep. On either side are submerged sandbanks that make it treacherous to sail through. The navigation is one part skill and two parts luck. Last time we tried to sail through it, we ran aground and had to wait for the tide to set us free. Right now, though, the tide is out and the channel is even shallower than before. Normally we would never risk it. But what choice do we have? In the open sea the warship would fill us with holes in a matter of minutes. Nobody says a word as we turn and head towards the gap between the two islands.

From the deck I look overboard and see right down to the sandy bottom all studded with starfish and coral. Slow, slow, says the navigator and with three men on either side to guide him, he tries to stick to the deepest path of the channel. In front of us, on the other side of the channel, the sea is a deep inviting blue. It is so close. And yet it might as well be a whole ocean away. Behind us, the warship appears around a bluff. It has followed even faster than we had expected.

'Veer starboard,' says one of our men. 'That's it. Nice and steady.' It is so quiet on our deck that you can hear the shouts of the commanding officer on the other ship; you can hear the wheels of the canons as they roll them into position. You can even hear the strike of flint as a match is lit.

'Can we go faster?' the captain urges. 'We are an easy target.'

'We must go slow,' insists Bart, an Englishman who was once a high-ranking navigator on a naval ship until he deserted. 'We cannot afford even one small error.'

And then the cannons start to fire and their shells fall down on us like huge balls of black rain. The air is filled with the smell of gunpowder and smoke and the surface of the sea turns from glass to a boiling froth.

'I can't see anything,' shouts Bart above the noise. 'Duck!'

One cannon ball passes straight through our main sail, tearing a huge hole before it smashes through the deck and into the hull. Maybe this wasn't such a good idea after all.

'Replace the sail,' the captain shouts, 'and then all speed ahead. Silas, come here. Now!'

While the rest of the crew are busy with the sail, I run up the stairs to the bridge. First he dismisses Bart, much to the navigator's annoyance, and then he places a wooden box in front of the wheel.

'You're young and lucky. You steer her.'

'Me?' I gasp. Another canon ball hits our ship on the starboard side just above the waterline, making the whole vessel shudder. The seamen start to panic.

'This is no time to argue with me,' he shouts. 'Just do it.'

'But!' I begin.

'Not another word or I'll throw you overboard.'

What choice do I have? I step up and take hold of the wheel with both hands but I can barely see over the top of it. The new sail is hoisted and fills with wind. We begin to pick up speed again. My hands are damp as I grip the vast wooden wheel. I turn it a little to the right and the ship veers sharply, throwing several men off their feet. Although the wheel is enormous it responds to the lightest touch. What am I doing, I ask myself? I have never steered a ship on the open sea let alone through a narrow channel. And yet if I make a single mistake, we will either be stranded on a sandbank or captured. Neither is an option.

I grip the wheel a little tighter and try to judge the depth by our distance from the shore. But it is impossible. I'm not a navigator. I am about to turn to the captain and tell him so, when I spot a dolphin leaping up ahead. I wipe both hands on my breeches and grip the wheel a little tighter. If a dolphin can do it, so can I.

I imagine the rudder below and see it cutting through the ocean like a fin and then I follow the dolphin's course, roughly of course. The dolphin flies through the water, easy, free, sure. Although we are not graceful and there is a moment when everyone stops and listens to the graze of our hull across a hidden sandbar, with a mixture of sheer luck and brazen bravado, I manage to steer my way through the channel. Finally the sea changes colour, from the palest turquoise to an endless dark blue, and we're in deep water again. Behind us, the warship has stopped firing. We're out of range. I watch the dolphin swim deep down into the blue.

'It's done,' I say, turning to Black Johnnie. He has both eyes tightly closed. He opens them and blinks twice, taking everything in. And then a broad smile spreads across his face.

'I couldn't look,' he admits. 'But I knew if anyone could do it, it would be you.' And then he lifts me down from the box and gazes at me as if he is about to embrace me. Instead, however, he clears his throat then gives me a manly pat on the back.

'Good show,' he says.

The warship is trapped on the other side of the archipelago of islands. It will take hours for it to sail around. At the end of the day, when we are many leagues from where they found us, I fall into my bunk. James has cried himself to sleep. Does he know, I wonder, what he has cost us? We could be lying low on our island, eating mangoes and roasting fish. Instead we almost gave ourselves away to be shot or hung, and our ship is taking in so much water that ten men have to bail day and night to stop us from sinking.

From where I'm lying, I can see a dull glint below his bunk. Lying on the floor is the lead box. It must have fallen down. The boy screamed blue murder when all the time it was right below him. He's fast asleep so I crawl underneath his berth and fetch it. I sit with it on my lap in silvery moonlight, examining it closely, turning it over and around. It is an ordinary lead box, solid, locked. Its brass hinges look a little more fancy than you might expect on a box this size. I run my fingers over them, idle and curious, then feel one shift slightly. There is a crevice carefully hidden behind the hinge, and out of it I pull a long brass key.

There is movement up on deck. Other crew members are still awake, bailing, repairing, sailing. Now is not the time. And so I return the key to its hiding place and gently position the box on the boy's chest. As I watch, his arms curl around it in his sleep.

# MARTINIQUE

We sail into St Pierre at dusk. In the sky behind us the sun is setting in streaks of red, orange and pale, pale green. The town is already dark but lit up with hundreds of flickering oil lamps and candles in windows. The sea that laps our bows is filled with colour and light. It shifts beneath us as if we are floating on a huge piece of Chinese silk.

Instantly, my heart starts to beat a little faster. All that my shipmates have talked about for hours is Martinique. About the tailor who makes fabulous clothes of the kind seen on the streets of Paris, the cobbler who makes the softest slippers, and the baker who makes the best bread in the whole of the Colonies. They have warned me about the old Figuier Quarter, where the streets are lined with rum distilleries and sugar warehouses, but where you risk being robbed at knifepoint after dark. They advise me instead to wander up the cobbled streets to the Cathedral, *Our Lady of the Safe Port*, in the upper town, a church that was built from money donated by several generations of pyrates and buccaneers, and where you must put a gold sovereign in the plate for luck. Up here, high above the harbour, are fountains, gardens and beautiful mansions built for the French, who came to the island and grew rich cultivating sugar cane. While they gaze down from their balconies, you can sit out in the cafés of the Place Berlin, drink coffee and eat crescent-shaped cakes all day long.

For the last few hours the men have been sprucing themselves up, shaving their faces with coconut oil soap and shaking the moths out of their clothes. The ship smells of the rosewater and the clove infusion that they splash over themselves. In truth, it doesn't make them smell any better. A good wash in fresh water would be more effective. Dressed up in satin and velvet embroidered with golden and silk threads, they would not, I tell them, look out of place in the Palace of Versailles in France. Although their faces are burnt deep brown by the sun, they still blush pink. I have nothing special to wear, but I hope to change that.

Using my share of the loot, I want to buy a red silk waistcoat and a pair of kid-leather shoes fastened with shiny brass buckles.

We drop anchor in the bay and, since I lost the ship's rowboat, we have to hail a couple from the shore to ferry us back and forth. After I have helped load the first with sacks of looted goods, boxes of coins and other trinkets, I step towards the second. But then I feel a hand on my arm.

'Not you,' Black Johnnie says. 'You stay on the ship with the boy.'

Naturally, I am astounded. For weeks, I have worked as hard as everyone else. And now all I want to do is to see St Pierre.

'What!' I say. 'But that's not fair.'

'You can go to the town tomorrow,' he clarifies. 'I'll take you myself. It's safer in daylight. Tonight, you must stay here. And that is an order.'

'And if I don't?' I retaliate.

He looks at me and raises his eyebrows.

'You swore allegiance to our code,' he says simply. 'If you disobey me, then I will regard your contract as broken. Like any of our crew who breaks the code, you will be put off as a mutineer. So you'll stay?'

Even though the fury still up boils inside me, I nod my head. What else can I do?

'Good,' he says.

And with that, he climbs into the first boat and sits with his back to me as they row towards the town. Safer for whom? I rage. I can look after myself.

James is sleeping in his bunk as usual. Right now, I wish that I hadn't spotted his stupid little head bobbing in the sea and brought it to the attention of the captain. I wish I had never set eyes on him.

The noise from the town carries across the water of the bay. I hear raucous laughter and the sound of smashing glass – bottles of rum, I'd guess. The noise doesn't lessen as the night gets later. In fact it gets louder.

Ever since our miraculous escape from the warship, nobody has mentioned how the boy with the box gave us away to the navy. They all talk as if we were the victims of bad luck. But I know that box is trouble. I need to know what's inside it and whether, as James insists, it holds the kind of treasure that would make others come after us. Now, while the ship is completely still, I see my chance. I slip out of my bunk and gently take the box from the sleeping boy's arms, replacing it with a box of tea one of the men was keeping under his bunk, and which might feel much the same if you were asleep. Then I push open the door to Black Johnnie's cabin, step inside and lock it behind me.

I light the candle, and look around. I have never set foot in here before – it is out of bounds to crew. The captain always hands his clothes and boots to me to wash and polish. I soon realise why. The room is a mess, the bed unmade and there is a pile of dirty clothes on the floor. Even boots I cleaned so carefully only the day before lie on their side under his bunk, the shine of the surface dulled by dust. Black Johnnie is always insisting on order and cleanliness. If the rest of the crew could see how he lived, they wouldn't take his orders quite so seriously.

The captain's table is covered in maps and books, coins and trinkets, quill pens and navigational instruments. A brass tin lies half-hidden under a pair of silk stockings.

I put down James's lead box, pick up the brass tin and open the lid. It holds nothing much – a handful of dirty rocks, souvenirs from somewhere special perhaps.

I turn back to the lead box and slide the key easily out of its secret cavity behind the hinge. It fits the lock and turns with a click. I push back the lid.

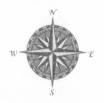

# AN UNEXPECTED VISITOR

Even in dull, flickering candlelight, the inside of the box overflows with colour. Reflected light dances across the cabin ceiling and the walls, red and blue and green. The sight is so beautiful that I gasp. I never knew such colours could be captured: the blue of a magpie's wing, the deep red of fine wine, the green of the western sky, just minutes before the sun goes down. I put my hand into the box and lift out dozens of jewels: rubies and emeralds and sapphires! No wonder kings and queens want to wear gems as fine as these. But these jewels have not been made into jewellery, they are still just smooth, glassy stones, carefully cut. Who do they belong to? They must be worth a fortune. A shipload of fortunes!

Johnnie talks about once, many years ago, finding a real ruby in an old shipwreck. It was sitting loose in a pile of coins. He traded that one jewel for a boat. In this box there must be a dozen rubies at least. No wonder McGregor wants it. No wonder he is willing to kill for it.

From somewhere close, I hear the faintest of taps. What if the captain were to find me in his cabin? I freeze and listen for the swish of oars approaching – But there's nothing, just the quiet breath of the boy asleep next door and the wash of the waves on the bow.

No, there it is again. A tap. I need to get out of the captain's cabin. In what I think is a stroke of genius, I swap the jewels with the dirty rocks, locking the lead box and hiding the key under a board in my cabin. If the box is stolen and the thieves can't unlock it, it might take a while before they realise they have the lead box but not the jewels.

A shadow crosses the porthole.

I put the brass tin where I found it under the captain's silk stockings and stuff the lead box into the waistband of my breeches.

As quietly as I can I climb the stairs to the deck. I slip along the bowsprit, where I can't be seen, and look out. No rowboats approach. The water is calm and undisturbed. There is a full moon and the night sky is scattered with stars. For a moment, my eyes are drawn to them. And then I see a figure is moving silently across the deck. Quietly, I slip back along to the foredeck, crouch down and watch. To my surprise it is a girl. She wears a pair of breeches and a vest, and her black hair is in two long pigtails, all sopping wet. She is slightly breathless, from swimming I guess. I relax. There is nothing to be frightened of. I stand up and step out of my hiding place, pulling myself to my fullest height.

'Miss,' I say. 'To what do we owe the pleasure of your company?'

She spins round and I see that she is Chinese. I bow to her.

'If you're looking for loot,' I tell her, 'then I'm afraid you're too late. They've taken it all to sell in the town. But may I offer you something else? A cool drink, maybe?'

Without a moment's hesitation, she leaps, hands first, and cartwheels across the deck. A blade flashes in her hand. Before I know it, she's right beside me, so close that I can smell the salt on her skin. The blade is cool against my neck. It's clearly not the loot she's after.

'What do you want?' I say, trying not to move a muscle.

'Box,' she says.

'A box?' I reply trying to sound puzzled. 'What box?'

She presses the blade a little harder.

'Box,' she repeats. 'Or you die.'

# OVERBOARD

The great bell of the *Our Lady of the Safe Port* strikes the hour, one, two, three. Maybe the men will soon be on their way back to the boat? But while the upper town is in darkness now, the lights of the Figuier Quarter are still burning. It looks as though I shall have to deal with this on my own.

'How about a box of biscuits?' I suggest. 'No weevils.'

The girl shakes her head. Then she presses the blade into my neck. A single drop of blood falls on to my hand. With one flick she could slit my throat.

'I don't have it,' I lie.

The girl steps in front of me and looks deeply into my face. And while her left hand still holds the knife, her right hand searches through my clothes, my shirt, my waistcoat, my breeches. She pauses and her mouth forms itself into a small smile – from my breeches she pulls the lead box. She smiles then pulls out a couple of lengths of muslin from her pocket and tears one in half with her teeth. She wraps the box tightly with a piece and ties its other end to her wrist.

I touch my neck. Luckily, the cut is not much more than a pinprick. Now the girl thinks she has what she came for, I'm hoping that she will go as quietly as she arrived. I take the smallest of steps back. Without even looking up, she aims her knife. I have no doubt at all that were she to throw it, she would be deadly accurate. I decide to take another tack.

'I won't say anything. I'll keep my mouth shut. You can go.'

She looks up at me and the whites of her eyes glimmer. For a tiny moment I think she will do it, she will just take the box and slip silently back into the sea. And then she smiles and even though it is a very attractive smile, I know that what will happen next will not be quite so pretty.

First she binds up my wrists with another length of muslin and then she marches me to the side of the ship.

Next she ties my ankles together. Then she takes a step back. 'Now jump,' she commands.

I take a look back at her. The knife in her hand is aimed straight at my heart.

'Jump,' she says again a little louder. 'Quick!'

From the corner of my eye, I catch a movement behind her. But it is only the boy. Even though I can't swim, I tell myself I should be able to wave my bound legs like a sea creature and float back up to the surface. I have a chance. I feel the knife point press into the small of my back. The girl is getting impatient.

'You want me push?' she hisses.

I don't. And so I take a deep breath and in the light of the full moon, I jump.

The ocean rushes to meet me and shoots up my nose, fills my mouth and roars in my ears. I open my eyes and see a million tiny bubbles, as if the stars above had fallen down to circle and illuminate me. Up above, the surface of the sea has closed over and is already lulling back to calm. At this point, I would not say that I am scared. Worried, maybe; concerned, yes. But although it sounds foolish, I am still a little smitten by the Chinese girl's smile.

I can just about make out the moon, undulating slowly, and the loom of *Tenacity's* hull. But both of them are getting smaller. I am not rising back up to the surface like a piece of driftwood the way I thought I would. No, I am slowly, but certainly, sinking. I glance below. In the light of the moon, beds of seaweed sway, their tendrils thick and slimy and so dark green they are almost black. One wraps itself around my ankle; I have to kick and kick to make it loosen and fall away. I start to sink a little faster. I strain at the binds that tie my wrists and ankles but get nowhere. The Chinese girl is as good at knots as she is at acrobatics. The harder I pull, the tighter they become.

My breath is almost gone. A bubble the size of a globe leaves my mouth and starts to rise to the surface. I feel the rise of panic. Silas Orr, I tell myself, you must do something. But what can I do?

My mind blanks and a series of faces appears: Black Johnnie, McGregor, Toombi, the lady on the boat, Ferguson, Catherine. My chest is about to burst and my head booms with pain. Agnes. I struggle against my binds but a blackness is starting to surround me. Will I ever see my sister again? Agnes – the word forms in my mouth as the last of my air rises upwards. But then all is suddenly clear. If I survive, I will go back. I will return to Scotland, to Agnes, with or without my fortune.

Suddenly I feel something grab my hair and give it a tug. And then I feel another, a harder yank that wrenches me upwards. It is so painful that I open my mouth and take in a gulp of water. Up and up I am pulled, hoisted by the hair, which is both astonishing and agonising until, with a final jerk, I break through the surface of the sea and take a huge gasp of air. Then I flail around with my bound hands until somehow I grasp something solid, the ship's ladders. I cling on to the wooden struts for dear life as my whole body is racked with coughing. Seawater is in my eyes, my nose, my mouth, my chest, and it is several minutes before I can breath properly again.

'You let her have it!' the boy shouts at me.

I touch my head. I am surprised that there is a hair still left. Every inch of my scalp hurts.

'No,' I say. 'I didn't.'

'Well, where is it!' he yells on the brink of tears.

'I swapped what was inside.'

The boy looks at me, unsure whether to believe me.

'All she got were some dirty rocks.'

He peers at me, still unsure.

'But it was locked! So where are they?'

'In the captain's cabin. They're safe, don't worry. Has the girl gone?'

He nods. 'I had to wait until she had swum a fair distance away. She might have heard me otherwise. That's why I took so long.'

'And where did you learn to swim like that?'

He looks at me as if I am stupid.

'My mother taught me,' he said. 'In the sea.'

Later, when he has cut through my bonds with a knife from the galley and helped me back on board the ship, he fetches some dry clothes, a flagon of rum and a goblet. I watch him concentrate on trying to pour the rum without spilling it. He's a queer little thing, much stronger than he looks. I decide to try a direct approach.

'Who was that girl?' I ask.

'I have no idea. Never seen her before in my life.'

I stand up. My legs are still a little shaky and for a second or two I think that they might give way. But then I regain myself.

'I almost died because of your box, James,' I tell him. 'So did you! So did the rest of the crew of this ship! You have to tell me what you were doing in the sea chained to a box full of jewels.'

He blinks twice and I realise that his eyes have filled up with tears. I wonder, for a moment, if I have gone too far. But then he looks up at me, and takes a deep breath in and out.

Then he tells me everything.

'You won't tell anyone, will you?' he says at the end.

I look at him in the dawn light and wonder how he has managed to keep his story bottled up for so long.

'Swear,' he says. 'In return for saving your life, swear on your mother's grave.'

'You have a mother?' a loud voice booms out. 'Would she like our new rowboat?'

Neither of us has heard the soft wash of oars approaching or the stamp of a boot on the rung of the ladder. Black Johnnie stands on the wooden railings above us. Below, one of our shipmates lies sprawled out while another tries to rouse him with a foot. I look over at James; he shakes his head, ever so slightly.

'Everyone had a mother once,' I reply nonchalantly. 'Except maybe you?'

Black Johnnie raises his eyebrows and then bursts out laughing. He has had a skinful of rum and maybe more.

'You will grow up to be a great wit,' he tells me. 'But use it wisely. Not everyone likes to be the butt of your jokes. Why on earth are you both awake? It's almost morning! Go to bed.'

As we are about to head back down to our cabin, Black Johnnie stops me.

'Why are you wet, Silas?' he asks.

'A late night dip,' I reply.

'And what happened to your neck?' he asks.

'I caught it on the rigging climbing out,' I say. 'It's nothing.'

He nods and slaps me on the back.

'Witty and brave,' he says. 'What else could a mother hope for?'

Once we are below decks, we climb into our bunks but I don't sleep a wink.

## ST PIERRE

At dawn, the crew are all fast asleep, their snores rising from their berths in a repulsive chorus. James lies flat out on his back, his eyes closed and both arms flung out above his head.

'Wake up,' I tell him. 'Come with me.'

We creep out of bed, up on to the deck and climb down into the rowboat. With an oar each, we row to town without anyone noticing. I ask around the docks and within an hour I have found a passenger ship leaving for Kingston, and spent one of my six doubloons on a ticket for James. He will be safer away from us and the jewels, and we may be safer without him. I promised him I would take the jewels to their destination, with or without the captain. But I am confident that I will be able to persuade Johnnie. There is a reward, James told me, that would make it worth our while several times over.

It is mid-afternoon by the time Black Johnnie finally gets out of his bunk. His hands tremble, his face is pale and his eyes are red. He's slept in his clothes, boots and all. After he's taken a glass of rum – to settle his belly, or so he says – he brings out a gong and bangs it to rouse the crew.

'Come on, lads,' he yells. 'We've got food stocks to pick up, rum to stow. Rouse yourselves. We sail on the tide tomorrow.'

'We do?' I ask. 'Where to?'

'West,' he says, 'I heard a whisper last night about a brig leaving Cancun with a haul of stolen Mexican silver.'

'But first...' he stands on the bridge, facing the town, shielding his eyes with his hand.

'You're going back to St Pierre?'

He sits down, heavily, on the step and rubs his face.

'We both are!' he clarifies. 'A promise is a promise even if my head aches and the world is far too bright for my eyes.'

'I don't mind if we don't go,' I tell him.

'Nonsense,' he replies. 'Besides, I have a few things I must collect. We'll take the rowboat. The cook will keep an eye on the crew. That is if he manages to open it. His eye, I mean. He drank enough to sink a schooner. Let me just fetch a few things.'

Ten minutes later he reappears on deck and, while he is giving orders to the cook, I slip down to his cabin and pocket the brass tin, just in case, I tell myself, just in case. I place the key to the lead box under the loose board by my berth, and turn to find Toombi there, pointing up to the deck: the captain is ready to go.

St Pierre smells of freshly baked bread and the molasses that they make from the sugar cane. The port is one of the busiest in the Colonies and the island is so rich that the English have tried to get their hands on it several times. Dozens of warehouses and shipping offices near the water are crowded with French seaman and dealers. But, away from the harbour, the streets are narrow and unpaved and there are flowers everywhere. Native women in bright dresses carry vast baskets on their heads like they do in Jamaica, and children sit in the shade of the banyan trees. Up above, the volcano, Mount Pelée, gently smokes.

'What do you think?' the captain asks me.

'It's beautiful,' I reply, 'but not as beautiful as Jamaica.'

He stops in his tracks and looks at me.

'But Kingston, my dear fellow, is a midden, is it not?'

I remember the slaves at the harbour. But also watching the blue of the bay below Ferguson's.

'A place has many different sides,' I reply. 'What about Scotland? Do you ever long to return there?'

He shakes his head.

'I like St Pierre more than Scotland,' he says. 'I like most places better than Scotland.'

'But it is your home!'

He looks down at the gentle ripple of the sea.

'My heart is my home,' he says with his hand on his chest.

I roll my eyes.

'If you must know,' he says, 'I was born in Cowgate in Edinburgh. But I would never call it home!'

I find this information hard to believe. The Cowgate, like Glasgow's Gallowgate, is a slum.

'I lived there until one day when I was about seven,' he tells me, 'I was plucked from the gutter by a spinster. She sent me to school. I was educated in the classics and was all set to inherit her wealth.'

'So what happened?'

'I met a man called Charlie and became a Jacobite,' he replies simply.

The brewer and his wife in Greenock who adopted me had often talked about the 'filthy Jacobites.' They had explained how these misguided fools believed a

French man, Charles Stuart, was the rightful heir to the throne. The more they went on about them, the more I began to like them. My adoptive parents had that effect on me. When they told me that the Jacobites had been crushed, I was deeply disappointed.

'Did you fight against the English?' I ask.

He cocks his head to one side and then he pulls up his shirt. A long white scar runs all the way from his left hip to the right side of his chest.

'I got this at Culloden,' he says. And then he turns and starts to walk up the hill.

'So, unlike you, my boy,' he calls over his shoulder, 'I have no home to go back to. In Scotland there is a price on the head of Jon Harkin.'

We walk to the upper town along steep alleyways lined with fancy shops. The market on the main square is packing up for the day and most of the shops are closing for lunch. We should have come earlier. As the sun blasts down and streets shimmer with heat haze, there is a sudden judder underfoot. Pots fall from balconies, fruit from trees and petals from flowers, but no one seems to take much notice.

'What was that?' I ask the captain. He shrugs and waves his hand in the direction of Mount Pelée.

'Just the mountain,' he says. 'It does that sometimes.'

Later we will visit the jeweller, but first Black

Johnnie takes me to his tailor. The rooms are cool and filled with rolls of silk, lace and velvet. Two lengths of white muslin hanging from the window frame flutter gently in the sea breeze. Black Johnnie has a new outfit to collect, a tricorn hat trimmed with feathers and a matching frock coat in pale blue.

'Very nice,' Black Johnnie says. 'Very nice indeed. And now, Silas, it's your turn.'

'My turn?' I reply.

The tailor has produced a small pile of clothes and is laying them out.

'I hope they fit,' Black Johnnie says. 'I had to guess the size. And I hope you like the colours.'

I try not to guess what the tailor has for me in case I'm disappointed, in case it's just a couple of hair shirts. But I have could not have chosen better myself. There are dark red velvet breeches, a green waistcoat, white silk stockings and even a pair of shoes with silver buckles. I am so stunned I don't know what to say.

'The boy doesn't like them,' says the captain. 'Never mind, we can order more.'

'No,' I shout out. 'I do, I do like them.'

'Well in that case, you better try them on to make sure they fit!'

The silk feels like cool water against my skin. The

velvet is as soft as the coat of a kitten. The shoes, although they are a little large, click as I walk to and fro. I love every single thing.

'Let me adjust,' the tailor says as, with a mouth full of pins, he crouches beside me and starts to fiddle with a seam. 'It needs to be a little more fitted.'

'Fitted or unfitted, he still looks a wonderful sight!' Black Johnnie says.

I stop in my tracks and look at the captain. His new frockcoat makes his face look browner and the blue of his eyes brighter. And then I tell him.

'I'll need them for when I go back to Scotland.'

He looks a little taken aback. The tailor keeps his head down and keeps working. Black Johnnie lets out a short sharp laugh.

'Why would you want to go back there?'

'Lots of reasons,' I shrug. I can't talk about Agnes now, not with the tailor listening.

The captain is shocked. He begins to pace up and down.

'It's true that buccaneering is fraught with danger, injury and the possibility of a premature death. Being a child wouldn't save you from the gallows. You'd swing along with the rest of us. You'd be safer in Scotland.'

He sits down heavily and sighs. 'As for me, I have a

wee stash. Maybe I should just retire before my luck runs out? But then again, it is not yet enough. Reason, sometimes, does not come into it.'

'I just need some money for my passage,' I tell him. In the cloth purse I still wear around my neck, I have five doubloons, but it is not enough.

'Of course.'

'I'll pay you back,' I tell him. 'All of it plus interest.'

'Don't think of it,' Black Johnnie replies. 'Besides, you have your share of the loot. Ask Bart for it. Aren't you going to try on the new breeches?'

As the captain averts his eyes, I undo the button and my old breeches practically fall to pieces as I take them off. I give the brass tin a quick rub with my sleeve as I put it into my new pocket.

In the cloth purse I still wear around my neck, I have five doubloons left: not enough for my passage home.

'Why don't you come too?' I suggest. 'It would be worth your while.'

But he isn't listening.

'A few more hauls,' the captain is saying. 'Seven or maybe eight and then I might be prepared to call it a day.'

I glance out of the tailor's window towards the bay then look again.

'Captain!'

'And what of the boy's box? We never did establish what was inside that was so precious. It might be worth a haul or two in itself.'

'Captain!'

Finally he looks up.

'What is it, Silas?'

'Our ship! It's gone!'

# DIAMONDS IN
THE ROUGH

The *Tenacity* has disappeared, along with the entire crew and what little there was left of our loot. We run down to the harbour and scan the horizon, as if the ship might still be there if only we look hard enough.

Nobody has seen anything. The harbour master claims he only speaks French and can't understand a word we say. And everybody looks at Black Johnnie and me in our fine new clothes with thinly disguised amusement. A pyrate without a ship is like a knight in armour without a horse: stranded, ridiculous, doomed.

When the church bell strikes six, the captain sits down on a barrel on the quay and holds his head in his hands.

'Why?' he repeats over and over. 'Why take my ship? The spoils, yes, but not the vessel!'

'Who do you think did it?' I ask.

'It can't have been the British Navy, not in French waters. And why choose my ship? There are dozens of others in the bay that are grander, bigger, newer.' He shakes his head. 'It must be McGregor. As an act of revenge for the *White Stag*. They must have seen me leave the ship earlier, and sent a raiding party.'

I am thinking that although McGregor has the lead box, and the *Tenacity*, he does not have the jewels and will not find the key under the board by my berth.

The captain suddenly stands up.

'Heaven forbid, my stash!'

'Your what?'

'I knew I should have brought it,' he curses. 'Ten years' work for nothing. It is all I own.'

'What did you say was inside?' I ask.

'A handful of white diamonds in the rough. One day I planned to get them cut and polished.'

I am suddenly filled with horror.

'They weren't valuable were they?'

He looks at me and laughs. But it is a sad kind of laugh.

'They were my fortune,' he says.

It seems the dirty rocks were not mere souveniers.

'I have money,' I tell him. 'Five doubloons. Take it.'

'Silas Orr,' he says. 'You are a true friend. You are the keelson in my heart.' I blush despite myself. The keelson is the length of timber laid along the keel of the ship to strengthen it. Black Johnnie shakes his head. 'Thank you for the offer, but it's yours,' he replies. 'Keep it safe.'

As the sun starts to dip into the ocean, he looks out, hopeless.

'Please,' I say. 'Please take the money.'

He shakes his head, no.

'I don't want money. All I want is my small brass tin. There's nothing I can do with a few coins.'

How can I tell him? How can I not? I open my mouth and then I close it again.

The captain doesn't notice. He is pacing to and fro – thinking of his diamonds.

'A solution has come to mind,' he says suddenly. 'We'll make chase.'

'In what?' I reply. 'We haven't even a tub to our name.'

First he glances round to make sure there is no one in earshot, and then he leans towards my ear.

'I'll win a ship at cards,' he whispers. 'I've done it before, I'll do it again. I'll use your doubloons for stakes.'

Black Johnnie holds my gaze as he waits for my reaction. I think he is more eccentric than I ever realised. But it's not the kind of thing you can tell someone. And then I see a possible solution that would suit both of us, if only the captain knew it.

'On one condition,' I tell him. 'If you win, you'll take me first to Scotland.'

His face falls.

'You ask a lot,' he says, as he mulls it over. 'It seems, my boy, that you are determined to return home. Normally I wouldn't entertain such an idea but what are my choices? Very well then, we have a deal.'

'Excellent,' I reply and hand him my bag of coins.

# A GAME OF CARDS

With the spring back in his step, the captain leads the way back along St Pierre's harbour. The light is turning pale pink in the west and the first stars are beginning to come out. As the sun dips, the colours of the sky grow deeper, richer. In all my time at sea, I have never seen such a beautiful sunset. And yet it feels ominous. The air is hot and heavy. A bad smell lingers in the back of the throat. My eyes blink with grit and ash. Above the town, the volcano churns out clouds of thick black smoke.

But the captain has other concerns. As we pass each tavern, he pauses and listens to the voices inside. Some are French, others Dutch. He keeps going until he hears the harsh rasp of English.

'Land ho!' he says with a wink.

This tavern is so dark inside that for a moment I can't see a thing. Slowly my eyes adjust and I make out a couple of long low tables, a girl with a filthy rag thrown over her shoulder, a plate of half-eaten fish, and, sitting beside a fire that cracks and spits in the corner, a small group of men. Each one is holding a mug of beer. There are cafés full of light and luxury in the upper town of St Pierre; this place is entirely the opposite. The captain and I, all dressed up our fine clothes, couldn't look more out of place. All conversations cease as, one by one, the men turn.

'Good evening,' Black Johnnie offers with a tip of his hat.

Their reply, if you could call it that, is the rasping of throats and the sound a mouthful of spit makes when it hits a fire. I don't like the look of them, not one little bit. I raise my eyebrow at Black Johnnie. But he pretends not to see.

'You been moored in Martinique for long?' he asks them after he has ordered us both a beer.

'Not long,' one of the men replies. 'Sailed in the day before yesterday.' He is dark skinned, wears a jacket with gold buttons and has black hair in a ponytail that reaches almost all the way down to his waist. By the look of him, the puff of his chest and the narrow glancing of his eyes, he is their captain.

Black Johnnie pulls out my stash of coins and pays with one. The girl with the rag shakes her head – she cannot break it – and he tells her to keep it to cover the whole evening's expenses. It is noticed. The men shift in their seats and catch each other's eyes.

'A good haul?' the man with the pigtail asks.

'That it was,' the captain replies. 'Our prize came from slavers.'

Throats are cleared, hands thrust into pockets and I suddenly have the strong suspicion that we are both about to be robbed and murdered. Black Johnnie's hand is on his dirk. The same thought must also be occurring to him. But instead of losing his nerve, he drinks his beer down and orders another.

'And to whom do we owe the pleasure?' he asks.

The men all glance at the man with the ponytail.

'Indian Tom,' he pipes up. 'You?'

'Jon Harkin,' the captain replies.

The light from the fire flickers over Indian Tom's face. He smiles. Two of his front teeth are missing.

'I heard you swung at Port Royal,' he says with unmistakeable pleasure.

'No, not me,' my captain says.

'You may be at liberty,' Indian Tom continues, 'but isn't there a price on your head?'

'A decent one, I hope,' Black Johnnie replies.

'I heard you robbed a merchant ship,' he went on. 'Burnt it too. The captain was none too pleased. Swore revenge.'

The captain's face freezes.

'Who told you that?'

Indian Tom smiles.

'McGregor and I are acquainted. I'd be on my guard if I were you.'

'What about you?' Johnnie asks. 'Have you been lucky?'

Indian Tom sniffs and then sticks out his left leg. Instead of a foot, he has a wooden stump.

'That is bad luck,' the captain says. 'To lose a leg.'

'Oh, no,' says Indian Tom. 'This was treachery, pure and simple!'

His eyes slide back and forth over his shipmates. As one, they look away.

'Let's all have a beer,' Black Johnnie says. 'I'll buy.'

This seems to cheer them up no end. He passes round a tankard each.

'A toast,' he says, 'to a common occupation, to our good selves, to Gentlemen of Fortune, no matter how lucky or unlucky we are.'

And yet he does not drink a drop himself. I see his technique – he takes his mug to the latrine full and returns with it empty.

When a game of three card brag is suggested, the men are all keen to play. The rules are simple; triples win, then pairs, then the highest card left.

I know he must be sober but my captain keels and blinks and sways in his seat like a drunk. He plays the first few rounds badly, betting on a pair of fours and losing a doubloon. Indian Tom laughs as he sweeps his winnings into his lap. Why bother robbing a man like Black Johnnie, his men must be thinking, when he throws his money away so easily.

After the eighth round I am beginning to worry. The captain has bet less but lost every single hand. He is down to our last doubloon. With a swig of his beer, he takes a look at his hand and flings his final coin in the pot. Everyone folds – everyone but Indian Tom, who raises the stakes with another coin and lays down his cards.

'A threesome beats a pair,' he tells Black Johnnie. 'You must give yourself up now, my friend.'

My small fortune, the first I ever had, is lost.

As Indian Tom begins to rise from the table, his pockets heavy with coins, Black Johnnie's hand shoots out and touches his arm.

'Wait,' he says. 'Another hand?'

'With what?' Indian Tom replies. 'You have nothing left to wager. Your fine clothes would not suit me.'

His men laugh. Black Johnnie forces a smile.

'I have rough diamonds,' he says. 'As big as my fingernail.'

'All my coins are not worth as much as that,' Indian Tom replies.

'Why not bet your ship and crew then?' Black Johnnie suggests. 'Just a thought.'

'Show me the diamonds!' he demands.

'Are you doubting my word?' Johnnie asks.

There is a moment when the only sounds are the crack of the fire and the distant cry of a night bird.

'Very well,' says Indian Tom. 'My ship. And all my men. A rough diamond.'

His crew gasp. Now here is a wager, they tell each other, that no one will ever forget.

'The victor will win both,' Black Johnnie clarifies. 'My boy here shall deal.'

And then he sits back down at the table and rubs his hands.

'When in doubt,' he whispers to me, 'do the opposite of what they expect.'

My captain carefully takes off his coat and hangs it off the back of his chair. He winces slightly as he does so – his shoulder has still not healed. It is a sign; this is where the real battle begins and ends, this is the moment he has been waiting for. And yet he doesn't have the diamonds. What will happen if he loses? I just have to hope that doesn't happen.

I slide on to a stool and pick up the cards. They are greasy and stink of tobacco smoke and sweat. I hold them in my hand and deal. Black Johnnie stares at his hand for an instant and swallows before he picks them up. I notice his eyes are closed when he holds them in front of his face. And then he opens them. A twitch of his lower lip suggests that they might be what he had hoped for. Indian Tom's face, however, reveals nothing.

At the bar, the pyrates are making their own wagers on who will win the game. I see the glint of coins changing hands and the glisten of sweaty palms. For a moment the two men are silent and I take a quick look at Black Johnnie's face. Although it is burned brown by the sun, his eyes are a pale, pale blue. I try to imagine him striding through Edinburgh, with its castle on a rock.

'Turn,' says Indian Tom. 'You lost the last hand, you must turn first.'

The captain runs a hand across his face and then he picks a card and slowly lays it down. It is the five of clubs. Indian Tom's eyes glint in the firelight as he slams down his own card; a five of diamonds. I turn back to Black Johnnie. He gives me a glance with the hint of a smile.

'Turn,' says Indian Tom.

He takes a deep breath and then lays down the next card. It is the five of spades. He has a pair. Indian Tom's men cannot contain themselves, cursing and whooping with equal measure. Black Johnnie sits back and wipes the perspiration from his brow. But it is not over yet and he knows it.

'Your turn,' he says.

Indian Tom takes in a lungful of breath and then slowly he lets it out. With a shrug he throws down his card. It is a five of hearts. Black Johnnie leans back in his chair.

'A draw,' he says. 'Then it all depends on the third card. The highest wins the hand.'

'The highest card,' repeats Indian Tom.

Rum is poured and this time Black Johnnie really drinks. The church clock on the hill outside strikes one.

'This time, let's change the order,' he suggests. 'After you.'

Indian Tom blinks several times. His eyes, although bloodshot, are black as two deep holes. He is both drunk and sober at the same time.

'Very well,' he says and slams down his final card on the table. It is a king of diamonds. 'Beat that.' Finally he smiles, revealing the wide space in his mouth where his teeth should be.

Black Johnnie's eyes well up but I can't tell if it is from relief or despair.

'Very well,' he says and tosses down his last card. It is an ace. The ace of hearts.

'I win,' he says simply.

Indian Tom's smile freezes on his face as he looks from the card to the captain's face and back again. And then he sits back and with a tiny shrug, exhales.

'Just as we stated at the start of the game, Ace is low. So *I* win.'

Black Johnnie blinks and then leans across the table and speaks softly.

'You jest,' he says. 'Everyone knows that in three card brag, the ace is high. A different rule was never mentioned.'

But Indian Tom just shakes his head.

'Men,' he says. 'You remember me stating the rule quite clearly?'

His shipmates, as one, swear that the rule was stated. They hustle shoulder to shoulder and come a little closer. Their hands rest on the hilts of their cutlasses. I see Black Johnnie's hand hover over his musket. But he would not stand a chance against so many. As he realises this, his shoulders seem to fall. His mouth has become tight. He will not meet my eye.

'A wager is a wager,' he says.

Before he can pull out his musket and turn this into a losing fight, I pull the brass tin out of my pocket and show it to them.

'Here,' I say. 'What's inside here is worth more than a fleet of ships!'

'Silas?' the captain says. 'You took my tin?'

'I did,' I say.

And yet it does not contain what Black Johnnie thinks it does. And I have given my word to James. I cannot let it go. Not here. Not now.

'Silas?' he asks again a little louder. Everyone in the tavern turns to look at me. This is worse, much worse than I could ever have imagined. What will Black Johnnie say when it is opened? A tear falls from my eye before I can stop it.

'It's all right,' the captain says quietly, patting me gently on the back. 'I forgive you. Just give it to me.'

Slowly, with a sinking inside my heart, I hand it over.

'I do love a hand of cards now and then...' Black Johnnie says, as he places the tin in the middle of the table. For a moment no one moves. And then Indian Tom reaches out. '...But not with a cheat like you, Sir!' the captain shouts. One hand grabs the tin and chucks it to me, the other grasps Indian Tom's wooden stump. With a yank he twists it up and over, throwing the pyrate off his chair, to fall flat on his face on the tavern floor.

The captain's hand is around my wrist and I am whisked through the tavern doorway and out into the night before the pyrates, their reactions slowed with too much rum and beer, can follow us.

'Run, Silas,' he yells at me. 'Run for your life!'

# TO THE SEA!

Outside, the dark is not dark anymore. St Pierre is lit up by brilliant bursts of orange that shoot out of the jagged lip of the volcano. The town seems to have woken up. Hundreds of people have come out of their houses to gaze up at Mount Pelée. They stand in their nightshirts here, there and everywhere, so we have to dodge left and right to avoid them as we run to the quayside. But whatever slows us down also slows down our pursuers who, judging by the shouting and the yelling of oaths, are a good deal more clumsy on their feet than we are.

'Almost there,' shouts Black Johnnie over his shoulder. 'If we can just make it to the rowboat.'

For what? I think. How shall we escape in a rowboat?

And then, like many moments in my life, everything seems to happen at once. The ground starts to shake violently underfoot. The road in front of me heaves up and splits. I am on one side, the captain is on the other. I realise I'll have to jump. I step backwards and my foot lands on something hard that crunches, like a snail shell. I look down and see that it is not a snail, but a huge black centipede, as long as both my arms put together. I let out a scream that is echoed by the high-pitched whinny of a horse in its stable. A dog starts to bark frantically and then yelps in pain. Up ahead, Black Johnnie has reached the jetty.

'Come on,' he shouts. 'Don't just stand there.'

I move to run forward and jump the crack, and a huge snake slithers right where I am about to place my foot. It has a brown and white pattern along its back; it's a fer-de-lance. One bite and I would be dead in under a minute. I freeze as it glides past a few inches from my left ankle, shimmering in the orange light, making its way as fast as it can towards the sea. Then I understand that the animals sense what the people have chosen to ignore. All around me, the broken cobblestones of St Pierre writhe with snakes, huge insects and whole colonies of red ants, all fleeing from the slopes of the mountain to the ocean.

I must jump the slowly widening split in the road, but I'm paralysed, watching the moving ground swarming with creatures. Black Johnnie is waiting ahead and the pyrates with their cutlasses raised are rounding a corner behind me. The captain seems to have stopped calling or maybe, I realise with horror, I just can't hear him anymore. The air is filled with the sound of screaming, both animal and human, as people, horses and dogs are bitten by terrified snakes.

A hand clamps my shoulder, a hand with the letters

# B -I -L -L

tattooed badly on the knuckles – a pyrate's hand. I turn. It is one of Indian Tom's men, a hulking thug with the look of a murderer. I am certainly done for now, I think. This is the end.

'Help me!' the pyrate yells, 'I hate snakes.' His eyes are wide and his whole body trembles. He has run faster than the others because he is even more scared than I am. I suddenly spot an opportunity.

'Will you help us in return?' I demand.

He would clearly sell his mother to get out of there.

'Anything,' he says.

'Swear on it,' I tell him

'I swear!' he repeats. 'But you've got to get me away from them!'

'This way, then,' I tell the pyrate. 'Follow in my footsteps, exactly.'

I take a deep breath and move. First we jump the crack. Despite the alarming shifting ground, it isn't as big as it looks. And then I take the next tiny step. A sidewinder zips past. And then an adder, swishing from side to side like a dancer. And then another. 'No sudden movements,' I tell the pyrate over my shoulder. 'No crying out. Your life depends on it!'

Step by step, we make our way through the sea of snakes: bright green pit vipers and enormous boa constrictors, red and yellow striped corals and more fer de lances. Several times a snake pauses and prods its head against my shoe. I look down at its forked tongue shooting out between the fangs in its mouth and am sure that my luck has run out. But I stay as still as can be, and the snake, with a small twitch, always moves on again, it is so intent on escape.

I can feel the shudders of my companion and hear his small groans of horror behind my back, but with me shouting more positive encouragement than I feel, we make it.

At the jetty, Black Johnnie is waiting with his musket drawn.

'No,' I yell out to him. 'He will help us.'

'Billy the Fiddle, Sir,' the pyrate shouts out. 'At your service!'

The captain cocks his head and frowns. Should he trust him? Probably not. On the other hand, a strong man might prove useful.

'Take out your weapons and put them into your kerchief,' he demands.

As fast as he can, the pyrate disarms; a cutlass, a small dagger, a heavy metal chain and a pair of knuckle-dusters. It is quite a haul.

'Take it all,' Billy the Fiddle implores. 'Just let me in your boat.'

'Very well,' the captain says. 'Hurry!'

The other pyrates have disappeared, chasing us forgotten in the scramble to save themselves.

As we run along the jetty, I glance down. Through the wooden slats I can see that the sand of the beach below has almost disappeared. Instead there is a shifting, wriggling carpet of snakes, insects and creepy crawlies, all heading towards the dark sea.

And so I am not watching my step when a fer-de-lance shoots in front of me. As soon as I feel it under my shoe, I jump back, but it is still too late; the snake rears up, both fangs bared, ready to strike. With a hiss, it spits a stream of venom into the air, then, as taut as a pulled rope, it weaves from side to side.

'Help,' I say, my voice little more than a whisper.

There is a sudden flash of light and a blast of noise. The snake twists straight upwards then falls down dead. Black Johnnie brandishes his smoking musket.

'Get in,' he shouts. 'Quickly, before you step on anything else.'

I have never been so glad to get off dry land in my life. Although snakes can swim, they cannot jump into a boat from the water.

'Can you manage to row on your own?' the captain asks Billy the Fiddle. 'I have an injury.'

'That shouldn't be a problem,' he replies.

After checking that there is nothing nasty below the bench, he takes the oars.

'Then row,' commands Black Johnnie.

Billy is strong and keen to leave: we shoot off at quite a pace. Black Johnnie rubs his shoulder. Even with an oar each we would never have been able to move at this speed.

Once we are out in the bay, Billy lifts the oars and turns.

'Where to?' he asks.

'To your ship, of course,' the captain replies. 'I won it fair and square. There was no rule that stated ace was low, was there?'

The pyrate shrugs. 'Ace is always high,' he admits, 'in three card brag.'

'Excellent,' Johnnie replies. 'And now I need to claim my prize.'

The ship, the *Curby Dodger*, is moored in a small cave just below the headland. Clearly Indian Tom wanted to arrive in St Pierre unannounced. Billy rows through a narrow opening in the cliffs that is all covered up with vines, and there she is, creaking slightly in the swell. Even in the near darkness of the cave, it is clear that the boat is a tub. One mast is slightly bent, the sails are ragged and the paintwork peeling. She is carrying so many barnacles her underside looks like the skin of a toad.

'There she blows,' shouts Billy the Fiddle, with more enthusiasm than the ship deserves.

We climb aboard. But how shall we sail her? Two men and a boy cannot handle a ship. A skiff bobs alongside filled with the pyrate crew from the tavern. This bunch must have set to sea instead of chasing us. I scan their faces. Indian Tom, I am relieved to see, is not among them.

'Where's the captain?' asks Billy. 'Is he with you?'

The crew all look a little shifty and shake their heads.

'We must have left him,' one says.

'He was right behind me,' says another. 'And then he wasn't.'

'Told us we'd swing if we didn't catch you,' says a third.

'Done it before, too,' says a fourth. 'Remember Tiny Nell?'

'And Finn the Pink.'

The crew have sobered up since the tavern. Needless to say, wherever Indian Tom is, stranded on the jetty or in the belly of a boa constrictor, he still has my silver doubloons. But I have the brass tin back in my pocket.

'I say, good riddance,' says one of Indian Tom's crew. 'The man's a murderer, a liar and a cheat.'

'And ace is high in three card brag,' adds another.

There is a moment when they look at us and us at them.

'It's just as well I'm here,' says Black Johnnie brightly.

'So what do you say, men?' says Billy the Fiddle. 'Shall we have a new captain?'

The crew glance at each other and sniff most unattractively. And then they murmur in agreement, no words as such, just a repulsive clearing of throats and a round of spitting.

'Jolly good,' says Black Johnnie with a faint smile, as they all come aboard. The captain continues, 'I run a tight ship. I'll need you all to sign an oath. And before we set sail I want you to check everywhere for unwelcome visitors – we don't want any vipers on board or...'

But he stops mid-sentence. Everything has fallen silent, the birds have stopped squawking outside the cave, drips are no longer falling from the roof, even the tide seems to have paused. I follow the line of Black Johnnie's gaze, turn and look through the mouth of the cave. On the flattened, dark surface of the sea is the rippling reflection of the fiery volcano. The smoke coming from its summit seems to have stopped. And then with a deafening boom and a vast plume of black, it erupts.

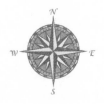

# THERE SHE BLOWS

The air is full of noise and ash and the roar of an explosion. The light is a strange shade of orange. The pyrates all just stand there with their mouths hanging open. 'Get below, cover your heads with wet rags,' orders the captain. 'Quickly! Now! Don't breathe the air.'

As I fall down the ladders, a scorching wind rushes into the cave, setting the rigging on fire. I throw my shirt in a barrel of water and pull it over my head. But still the heat and smoke burn my lungs. Everyone is screaming, for help, for God, for their mothers.

'Silas? Silas!' It is Black Johnnie, his hand around his mouth, his eyes searching frantically for me.

'Here,' I say and hold out my hand. He staggers

towards me, falls down and passes out. And then everything goes black.

When I come to, it is light – not the bright clear light of the Caribbean but the murky light of a Scottish afternoon. The captain is sprawled beside me, his brand new hat over his face. The tricorn is tattered and burnt, the feathers gone. Tentatively, I lift the hat. To my relief he is still breathing.

'Captain?' I whisper. 'Wake up.'

He blinks and then sits up, looks around and then falls flat on his back again.

'This is just a dream,' he mumbles to himself, 'a bad dream.'

But it isn't a dream. I leave him and climb the ladders to the deck. We are at sea, a mile from the shore. We must have been washed out of the cave by the great waves that follow an eruption. The *Curby Dodger* may have looked bad before but now she is a charred shell of a ship, the decks scorched, the masts gone. At least, I tell myself, we are still afloat. Others were not so lucky. The water is filled with the broken remains of boats and houses.

I look towards Martinique but St Pierre is no longer there. The town has been completely swept away, buried beneath a river of molten lava. The ruins of the distilleries, their warehouses once stocked up with rum, now burn out of control. But elsewhere, nothing moves. Who could survive such a catastrophe? Only the afternoon before I had walked through the town's handsome streets. And now the French bakeries and the pleasure gardens, the fine church and the grand squares are all gone.

'What a sight.' Black Johnnie stands beside me. 'What an awful sight.' Tears well up in his pale blue eyes.

Most of the pyrates seem to have survived. Three are missing and one stayed on deck and had all his clothes scorched off his back, but with lots of rest and cooling seawater poultices, he looks as if he will live. The others huddle in groups and share their smokes. As they run their fingers along the charred timbers of the deck it is not hard to work out what they are thinking. They will jump ship at the first opportunity, if, that is, we don't run aground or sink first.

We drift in the current away from the devastated island of Martinique and into the open sea like a piece of flotsam. The ship has stores of dried meat and biscuits and several barrels of rum. The men, with nothing to do but sit and wait for something to happen, get drunk.

I find the captain on the ship's foredeck leaning on the charred rail watching the water.

'Are you all right?' I ask.

He shakes his head.

'Silas,' he says. 'We are in a dire predicament. I do not see how we will come through. We had hoped to chase the *Tenacity* if I could win a ship, but this one is no longer sea-worthy. We are at the mercy of the wind and the tide, the moon and the stars. Who knows when and where we might wash up? We must prepare for the worst.' He is silent. And then he pats me on the shoulder. 'If we survive this, at least we still have my stash. You have my brass tin, don't you Silas?'

'I...' I begin.

'You don't need to explain', the captain says, 'I forgive you.'

I swallow before I speak. This is going to be harder than I ever realised.

'I have the tin, Captain,' I reply, 'but I do not have the stash.'

He looks at me long and hard, not quite understanding.

I pull the brass tin from my pocket and hold it out. He takes it and, still watching me, opens the lid.

# JAMES'S STORY

The stars are out tonight, lighting up the sky with their bright scattering. It would be a perfect evening if all was well. But I don't think that anything will ever be the same again.

'Where did these come from?' Black Johnnie asks softly.

'From James's lead box,' I say. 'I'm truly sorry about your stash. I didn't know what it was. I needed the tin, you see.'

'Only kings and queens have this sort of treasure. And gentlemen of fortune, perhaps. And so you...'

'I swapped the contents, yes.'

The captain inhales sharply.

'But we can't keep them. I promised James we would

deliver them – and collect the reward, of course. I gave my word. Otherwise he wouldn't have gone home to Jamaica. It seemed like the perfect solution. I could see my sister in Glasgow, win a grand reward. And help him.'

'You sent the boy to Jamaica? When?'

'I bought him a passage yesterday morning,' I tell him, 'before you and I went to St Pierre, before everything happened.'

Now that time seems an age away.

'A clever move,' Black Johnnie says. 'Not one that I had authorised, but, nevertheless, at least he is safe. Well done.'

A fight breaks out down below and we stop talking for a moment. There is the crack of glass, a bottle breaking on something hard – a head perhaps. This is followed by a chorus of oaths, not, as you might expect about the welfare of the head, but fury at the waste of rum. And then, as suddenly as it all began, the men quieten down again and one of them begins to sing so softly it sounds, from here, like a lullaby.

'So tell me,' the captain asks, 'what are these jewels the boy was chained to, and where did you promise to deliver them?'

I take a deep breath. This is not going to be easy.

'They're called the Jewels of Caracas,' I say. 'We

have to take them to a man in Glasgow called William Dunlop.'

Black Johnnie raises his hand.

'Stop,' he says. 'Did I hear you say "we"?'

'You said you'd take me if you won a ship. Remember?'

He shakes his head and a smile plays across his lips.

'And I know what you're thinking,' I say. 'Why not just keep the jewels?'

'The thought did occur,' Black Johnnie says.

'I gave my word to James.'

He waits for more. I have no choice but to explain.

'I swore I wouldn't tell his story to a soul, but...'

'Generally I would advise you to keep a promise,' the captain says softly. 'But generally I am not adrift in the sea holding a king's fortune in my hands.'

And so I tell him how I found the key to the lead box and then unlocked it. How I swapped the contents of the lead box with the brass tin. How the Chinese girl took me by surprise and how I almost drowned. How I persuaded James to go home so he could not lead others to the jewels. And finally, how I had made the boy tell me everything.

'And what a story it was,' I say.

'Well, go on,' the captain says. 'Tell me. From the beginning.'

James told me that his mother, Isabella, was the daughter of the Duke of Rothesay. She was not only wealthy, she was also so beautiful that men fell in love with her all the time. Her father wanted her to marry well. He had no male heirs and didn't want his money to fall into what he called 'the wrong hands'. But when she was nineteen, Isabella fell in love with a sailor and eloped. Only a few months after they were married, the sailor had to go back to sea and shortly afterwards she heard that his ship had been caught in a terrible storm and broken up. None of the crew was found among the wreckage. All were presumed drowned.

Isabella was left widowed and expecting a child. Her husband had left her nothing but a few strange pieces of treasure. There were some foreign gold coins, some Spanish silver, and, most spectacular of all, the so-called Jewels of Caracas. They were not what you would expect to find in the possession of an ordinary sailor.

'He had links with pyrates,' said Black Johnnie, listening closely.

'I think so,' I say.

James had told me that the Rothesay family had kept Isabella's short marriage a close-guarded secret. Her father took her back into the family home on the condition that when James was born six months later, he was to be passed off as the son of a lady's maid. Her father intended to marry Isabella to the first respectable man who came along. But she wasn't interested in suitors. She spent as much time as she could with her baby. She played with him and read to him and loved him so dearly that he always knew who was his real mother and who was the maid.

When the pressure from her father to marry became intolerable, Isabella decided to leave Scotland and the family home. She told her father she would manage the family estate in Jamaica and, without waiting to hear his many objections, sailed with James and her trusted maid to the Colonies. Here, they lived an idyllic life in a great white house, swimming every day in the blue sea and managing the plantation. Isabella had decided that she didn't want to use slave labour; she wanted to pay her workers and make provisions for their welfare. Her friends and neighbours were outraged, her father furious at the downturn in his profits.

'I like the sound of her,' says Black Johnnie.

'Stop interrupting,' I tell him.

'Sorry,' he says. 'Go on.'

Even tucked away in Jamaica, Isabella received many offers of marriage – from locals with ambitions, from Americans with great fortunes, and from bankrupt British lords. Every one was turned down – she told

James that she'd never met a man who could compare with his father, the sailor she had loved so completely. And yet the duke told her he would not support her forever. She would have to find a husband soon or return to Scotland to enter a convent. That would mean leaving James forever.

One fateful day earlier this year, James had been present when Isabella received a letter – yet another proposal – this time from a wealthy shipbuilder back in Scotland. She laughed as she read out the letter to James and the maid, and made fun of this poor chap who signed himself William Dunlop. Then she came to a line of Shakespeare in his letter.

> Nothing of him that doth fade,
> But doth suffer a sea-change
> Into something rich and strange.
> Sea-nymphs hourly ring his knell:
> Hark! now I hear them – ding-dong bell.

This made her stop abruptly, and she seemed wholly distracted for the rest of the day. That night, James woke in the wee small hours and saw his mother pacing from her room to the veranda and back, pausing occasionally to write feverishly in her journal, then rising to pace again.

The next day she called James to her and said that this letter writer, William Dunlop, knew a line of poetry that was very important to her. This man might somehow be James's father, or perhaps might have known him, or might be an imposter, trying his luck. She said she would send Dunlop a gift and whatever he did with it would determine who he really was, and that would decide her answer to his proposal.

'But he might be the wrong man. And he might keep it?' James pointed out. It was a huge risk.

James had never seen her looking so desperate. After a sleepless night, her eyes were red and her face pale. The outcome would determine not only her life, but his. It was their one chance.

Isabella and James locked the jewels in the plain lead box with the concealed key and drove to Kingston to find a merchant or naval vessel that would ship them to Glasgow. She had decided on a payment of one hundred gold pieces for the safe passage of the box. The next merchant ship bound for Glasgow was McGregor's. He agreed to take it but when James met McGregor he felt deep distrust. So much depended on this box for both of them and so, when the ship was just about to depart, James left his mother a note and slipped away. With no idea of what he was letting himself in for, he crept on board the boat and hid among the cargo.

'The night before we raided the *White Stag*,' I told the captain, 'McGregor found James sitting by his mother's box. He forced the boy at knifepoint to open it and, having seen what was inside, realised that this was no ordinary piece of cargo. He shackled the stowaway to the box with a chain , forced him to wear a cork jacket, and when we stormed the ship he threw them both into the sea.'

'He wanted the jewels for himself?' Black Johnnie said.

'Oh no,' I replied. 'That wasn't his plan. He knew that the jewels could only be a pyrate's haul. He planned to deliver them to Dunlop and demand far more than Isabella's reward in return for not exposing either of them to the authorities.'

'A blackmailer. And now,' asked the captain, 'as well as my ship, McGregor thinks he has also stolen back the box, and the jewels?'

'He does. And I expect he will head for Glasgow and follow his original plan.'

'What a story,' says Black Johnnie. 'What a child. What a villain!'

'But then,' I point out, 'Dunlop will open the box and find your rocks.'

Black Johnnie frowns.

'He will not recognise them,' he shrugs. 'He will fail Isabella's test.'

We sit on the deck in silence for a moment.

'We are in no position right now to take anything anywhere,' the captain says. 'But if our luck changes, we could head in the direction of Glasgow as I agreed.'

I keep my mouth shut. I don't want him to see the curl of my smile, not yet, at least.

'You have given your word to the boy. And I know you want to see your sister. And also, we might be able to claim the reward – a hundred gold pieces is a small fortune – and reclaim my stash and then follow my ship to somewhere where we can storm her and take her back.'

'The eruption will have blown them off course,' I point out. 'If we make haste we could get there before them.'

He pauses to think. 'You know, don't you, Silas, that in Scotland there is a price on my head. I would not be able to stay long.'

'Fast in, fast out, as you always say.'

'Fast in,' he agrees. 'And very fast out.'

# A FRESH
# START

We talk for hours while the boat drifts on the current, then fall asleep on deck. The next morning, the captain gets to his feet and stretches. He shouts below deck, 'Time to get to work, men! Billy! Rouse the lads.'

Half an hour later, the men squint in the harsh daylight. They look crumpled and cross and even uglier than they did before. Johnnie stands on what was the bridge and points to a speck in the distance.

'About a mile to the port of our boat is a small island,' he says. 'I want each man to take an oar, or, if not an oar, a length of wood – anything that they can paddle with.'

Not one of them moves. They look at Black Johnnie as if he has lost his mind.

'It's far too far,' one says. 'We'd never reach it.'

'Do as your captain says!' roars Billy the Fiddle, which makes every one of them jump. Grumbling, they pick up what they can find. I have a sudden notion that they might use them to club us to death.

'Good men,' says Black Johnnie. 'As you can see, our predicament is dire. All it will take is one small storm and we shall lose the boat and probably our lives.'

The men shuffle their feet and stare blackly at the deck. One or two of them shrug in agreement.

'Now I am not ready to enter Davy Jones' locker quite yet,' he goes on. 'Trust me and we shall all live to go on account many times more. Listen carefully. I have a plan.'

With all the men in the rowboat and the *Curby Dodger* roped behind, Black Johnnie's plan is to tow the boat to the island. But it is backbreaking work; the boat is heavy and old and the currents are strong. Many hours pass and we seem to have made barely any headway at all. Bolstered with the promise of extra rum and biscuits, however, the men plough on. By late afternoon we finally reach the island and drop anchor in a small sandy bay surrounded by palms.

I jump down from the bow of the ship and wade to the shore. The sea is deep blue and the sand is white. It looks like paradise. And yet I feel uneasy and don't know why. Is there something or someone watching us?

I'm leaning down, trying to catch a fish in a shallow stream when a shadow falls across the water. Two black legs stand on the other side of the stream. The sun is in my eyes but I can see is that it's a man, a tall, muscular, black man holding a crudely made spear. He raises it. I gasp and tense, ready to feel the point through my neck. He releases the spear and it flies forward, straight through the body of the fish. The man laughs and throws open his arms.

'Toombi!' I cry.

He is as pleased to see us as we are to see him. After jumping off the *Tenacity* when he realised it had been commandeered by McGregor, he swam all the way to the island and had no idea how long he would likely remain.

'So where are they headed?' Black Johnnie asks Toombi.

Toombi mimes the lead box and then he points east.

'What did he say?' the captain asks.

'They're taking the lead box to Scotland,' I explain.

Toombi holds up a finger and then snakes it back and forth.

'But slowly,' I say. 'The crew are taking their time.'

'Excellent,' the captain says.

For the next few days we cut down trees and hoist new masts, we make sails from anything we can find – hammocks and sheets and even the shirts from our backs – and weave rigging from rope made from jungle vines. We heel the ship over and scrape the barnacles and seaweed from the keel. On board I polish every handle, every brass ring and hook with the juice of a soursop fruit until they shine. As well as plentiful fish, the island has a population of wild pigs and abundant fruit trees. Every night we eat roast pork or fish followed by roast pineapple.

Once the wood is sealed with pitch and rubbed down with tallow, the *Curby Dodger* looks much better than she did before. The men, too, seem to have changed. A diet of meat, fresh fruit and hard work has put them all in fine spirits. They have a new-found respect for Black Johnnie. Their skin, so nearly lost on Martinique, has been saved.

'So where first?' asks Billy the Fiddle. 'To Jamaica, maybe Caracas, or we could head to the Dry Tortugas to await passing trade?'

Black Johnnie smiles and shakes his head.

'Not there,' he says.

'You want to go to the American colonies?' Billy frowns. I know he is thinking that the *Curby Dodger* is much improved but with makeshift sails and rigging made from vines, a destination so far away could be overambitious.

'Wrong again,' the captain replies.

'So where to?'

Black Johnnie takes a deep breath. He is about to speak but then offers a slug of rum instead.

'Scotland!' Billy the Fiddle bellows when he hears what the captain plans. 'Not on your life!' And he launches into such a volley of oaths that I am tempted to cover my ears.

The captain takes Billy aside and gives him what he calls 'an advance guarantee' for himself and the crew. It is the smallest of the Jewels of Caracas, a slender purple stone that sparkles like a chandelier. Billy's eyes widen.

'We can ask the crew,' he says. 'But I wouldn't build your hopes up.'

The crew's reaction is similar to Billy's.

'Impossible,' one of them says.

'A suicide mission,' says another.

'If successful, you will earn an ample reward,' the captain tells the crew. 'It might be more than you could earn on the high seas in ten years.'

'Why don't you just sell whatever this is you're delivering?' one of them asks. 'And split the profit?'

'Perhaps it will come to that,' the captain agrees. 'But let us first try my plan. As well as personal reward for each and every one of you, it is an honourable quest. The fates of a young boy and his mother are in our hands. How can we forsake them?'

The men grunt and spit and fart and swear.

'Toombi?' I ask. 'Will you come?'

He nods his head vigorously.

'Well, that's one,' says Black Johnnie hopefully.

'Shall we?' Billy the Fiddle asks the others. 'Shall we follow the captain's plan?'

'We follow *you*,' one says, and the rest nod in agreement. It is clear they trust him more than they trust Black Johnnie.

Billy the Fiddle scratches his head. And then he looks east.

'It is at least two months at sea,' he says. 'But if we take the Great Circular by the way of Halifax, Nova Scotia, with decent supplies and a wind at our back and with hard work and a rationing of rum, it wouldn't be impossible.'

'Well?' Black Johnnie asks.

'I say we sail on the next tide,' says Billy the Fiddle. 'To Scotland!'

'To Scotland!' the crew reply in unison.

# A SUDDEN SQUALL

Our route is to be up the coast of America to the far north to catch a westerly trade wind, which, with a bit of luck, will carry us all the way. Billy the Fiddle, despite his appearance, knows more about how to read the stars and plot a map than our own navigator on the *Tenacity*. He has all the instruments, an octant and sextant, which use the stars to work out latitude, or distance from the poles. For longitude, or how far east or west we are, he uses a compass and 'dead reckoning'. Every day it is my job to throw a wooden beam on a rope into the sea at the bow of our ship and record how long it takes to reach the rear. With that, he tells me, he can calculate our speed.

Unfortunately, most of his shipmates have less

experience of the open sea, preferring to anchor in safe harbours at the least hint of a storm. What makes matters worse is that they have little inclination to learn, and prefer to spend their time below decks playing cards, sleeping, or, at a push, helping the cook prepare our meals. I soon realise that any pyrate with sailing experience, after a passage aboard the *Curby Dodger*, had a habit of not coming back after shore leave. It is a miracle that the ship has lasted this long. Others with more experienced men and in better shape lie at the bottom of the sea.

I volunteer to learn the ropes and, with Billy's help, find out how to coil a line and reef a sail. I memorise the names of ropes, the halyard that raises the sails, and the cunningham that lowers them; the sheet that trims the sails and the painter line, which is used to tow the dinghy. Next, I learn to tie knots: a bowline, a clove hitch, a reef knot and a rolling hitch. 'These will save your life,' Billy tells me more than once, and then he makes me practise over and over, though I show him I can tie them perfectly well already.

With the wind at our back, we sail north, keeping close to the shore to avoid being spotted by any merchant ships. For four days the voyage goes well. The wind is steady and the surface of the sea is tipped with white and skimmed by flying fish. Dolphins dive in front of our bow and a pod of sperm whales passes by so close that the spray from their blowholes showers down on our decks like rain. And then, just off the coast of Florida, the air turns a strange yellow colour, the shadows are violet and a bank of cloud looms up ahead. Billy the Fiddle licks his finger and holds it up to catch the direction of the breeze. He frowns.

'Is everything all right, Bill?' asks Black Johnnie.

Billy the Fiddle shrugs his great shoulders.

'Probably just a squall,' he says.

The rain falls softly at first but then begins to pound down on the surface of the sea. The pyrates put down their cards, crawl out of their hammocks and come up on deck. Here, they take off their clothes and use the shower to wash themselves, singing and hopping from leg to leg as they pull off their trousers and soap up their hair. So I'm laughing when the first gust hits the ship, snapping half a dozen ropes and sending one man over the side without a stitch on. As we're pulling him back on board, a huge wave breaks and hisses as it races by. Up above, the sails strain and threaten to tear. No one's laughing anymore. The captain's face is pale.

'We're being tossed like a rag,' he shouts.

'We need to reef the mainsail,' shouts Billy. 'Before it's in tatters.'

The sails need to be pulled smaller so they don't

catch the full force of the blast and tear. Some of the clewlines and the buntlines, the ropes that we use to hoist the sail up to the yard, being handmade from forest vines, have frayed and broken, so I volunteer to go up the mast and bundle the sail into the gaskets or ties. I shimmy up the rigging to the main yard, edge my way along, and start to haul. The sail is sopping wet and much heavier than I had expected. As the wind blows hard and harder still, it is all I can do to hold on. The waves come faster now, rank after rank of them, each one hitting us with a huge boom.

Rain is streaming down my face and into my eyes as I grab handfuls of sail, haul it up and secure it with a knot. The ship lurches from side to side, each time dipping so low that that I can almost touch the cresting waves with my hand.

'Come on, boy,' yells Billy from below. 'Faster!'

But my hands are cold, my arms are getting tired and the sail keeps slipping out of my grip. Once again I watch as it unrolls from its binding and flaps loose. All my fancy knots, I realise, count for nothing.

'I can't do it,' I cry out.

And then I catch sight of a figure in the corner of my eye.

'Ready,' a voice calls out. 'One, two, heave!'

The captain has climbed up beside me, his fine white

shirt stuck to his body and his hair in coils. With both my arms and his one good arm, we haul the sail up and over and, once I have tied them, he pulls each one of my knots as tight as they will go.

'Good lad,' he says. 'Almost there. Now the next one.'

But we are still too late. The sea surges, the wind hits us with huge force and below us, what's left of the mainsail rips right down the middle.

The last thing I remember is a stream of oaths from the captain. When I open my eyes a few seconds later, the world is upside down and I am racing forward, headfirst, towards the churning black sea. And then, with a jerk that pulls every single muscle in my body, I come to a stop. My left ankle is burning almost more than I can bear. It takes a second or two to understand what has happened. I have fallen off the mast and am dangling by my leg from the loop of one of the ropes that I used to tie the sails.

Several thoughts race through my head, none of them good: the rope will snap or my knot, a clove hitch, will loosen and untie. As the boat climbs mountains of swell and pitches down the other side, I swing from one side to the other, back and forth, passing high above the deck and the sea, then the deck and the sea again, and I hear the crew's shouts below. I pass by the mast, so close that I can smell the black tar that protects it from the salt water. And then I feel a tiny tug and then a bigger one. I glance up and high above I see Black Johnnie lying at the very end of the yardarm with both hands on my rope, his face strained with effort as he pulls.

'Got you,' he says when at last he has a hold of my foot. 'I always knew you were a lucky blighter.'

I swing around and catch hold of the yard with both hands. And then, arms and legs trembling with effort, I shuffle along until I reach the main mast.

'Grab hold,' shouts the captain. 'Then use the rigging.'

I have never, I swear, held a mast as tightly as I do now. My face, my clothes, my hair are covered in tar. Then slowly, slowly, I climb down the rigging to the decks with Black Johnnie not far behind me.

'See, I told you,' says Billy the Fiddle as he helps me on to the deck. 'I told you a good knot could save your life.'

Even if I had been faster with my knots around the sail, it is doubtful that it could have been saved. Only one spanker on the mizzenmast is still in one piece. The rest – the topsails and the topgallant sail, the skyrail and the jibs flap – are in shreds. The squall dies down almost as quickly as it began. The sun shines through the clouds, and through the holes in the tattered sails.

We sit, the captain and I, on the decks and stare out

at the sea, which is now calm again. The captain still has the rope that held me in his hands. Without a word he passes it to me. The knot has held but the hemp is frayed. Only a few strands are left.

The captain's face is white and drips with sweat. When he stands up, he winces with pain and clutches his shoulder.

'Are you hurt?' I ask.

'Shipshape,' he replies. 'It is just the shoulder that is still bothering me.'

A spot of blood has appeared on his shirt and is beginning to get bigger. The captain swallows and looks as if he might faint.

'I think I need a surgeon,' he says.

'Land ho!' yells Billy the Fiddle.

The captain frowns into the distance. According to our plans, we should be heading past the Carolinas by now, but the squall has blown us right off course.

'All hands on deck,' the captain commands. 'We make for the shore. Whichever shore that may be.'

# THE
# MANGROVE
# SWAMP

The coast is like nowhere I have ever seen before. The land is not land at all but a swamp with still, stagnant water, thick sea grass and small, stunted trees. There is nowhere to dock and so we drop anchor in the mouth of a wide estuary. Toombi volunteers to stay and look after the ship. A few others join him. I don't blame them. This land is hardly what you'd call inviting. We take the rowboat, and paddle up one of the hundreds of narrow channels that seem to lead inland. After the roar of the sea, my ears strain in the silence. The only things I can hear apart from the constant dripping of water are the buzz of mosquitoes and the cries of strange birds. I don't like it. Not one bit.

I turn and look at Black Johnnie. His eyes are open

but only just. A pad of linen on his shoulder is soaked with blood again. He notices me staring and he gives me a small smile.

'This won't take long,' he says. 'We'll be back on course to Scotland before you know it.'

A surgeon will fix him, I tell myself. But what if we can't find one? And even if we do, how can we pay him? And what if he refuses to treat a pyrate and hands him over to the magistrates instead?

'Where are we going?' I ask Billy the Fiddle.

'One of the men has been here before,' he tells me. 'He is sure there's a settlement round here somewhere.'

I turn and look at my crewmates. A man with only a few rotten teeth in his mouth and a ring through his ear looks at me with a shifty expression.

'Just up ahead,' he says and points with a finger covered in warts. 'It's right in the middle of the swamp.'

If it were up to me, I wouldn't trust him an inch. He may be leading us straight into an ambush or round and round in circles.

But then he lets out a short, sharp cackle. There's a goat's skull on a stick.

'I knew it was here somewhere,' he says.

We round a bend and the water stretches out into a scummy lagoon. On the far side is a cluster of a dozen ramshackle huts on a spit of land. A couple of stray dogs start to bark when they see us but nothing else stirs. Finally, just before we reach a tumbledown jetty, a man in a filthy frock coat and tricorn hat comes out of one of the huts clutching a musket.

'Scarlet pantaloons!' shouts the man with the rotten teeth.

I must look as astonished as I feel, because he explains: 'It's the password. This isn't a place you can find on a map. But those who know it call it Skull Creek.'

The man in the frock coat puts down his gun and urges us to throw him a line, which he ties on to the jetty. He is English, by the sound of him, but his skin is a leathery brown colour. He clasps the man with the rotten teeth like a brother, which is what, in fact, he is.

'Long lost but dearly missed,' he says and they both laugh so hard that more teeth might be lost before they know it.

A hut is found that we can sleep in, and that night, in celebration of our visit, a hog will be roasted and some bottles of wine opened.

'Only the finest of French,' our host assures us. 'From a French galleon that ran aground on the Keys. Unless you'd like rum from Jamaica. Or gin from London. It may not look like a great place to drop anchor, but in Skull Creek we have anything a man could wish for. Except women, that is.'

Unfortunately there are no surgeons either.

That night the captain falls into a delirious kind of sleep. His head is burning hot and his body is damp with sweat. I am not in the mood for dancing but I know that the men will stay up drinking until dawn. And so I take my place beside Black Johnnie and fall asleep to the sound of smashing bottles.

'Silas?' I wake at the sound of my name. It must be hours later. The captain is sitting up on the rough hemp we have been given for a bed. His eyes are shiny but his face is deathly pale.

'Look at the moon,' he says.

I look up through the cracks in the roof.

'I see it,' I reply.

'How I love this world,' he whispers.

The lagoon is surrounded by a fringe of trees whose branches hang down into the water. In the moonlight it looks even more foreboding than during the day.

'There's so much more to see,' he says softly. 'The ice flows of Nova Scotia. The palaces of France, the lush forests of the Azores. I am sure you will see them all. One day.'

A lump rises in my throat. What does he mean?

'But you'll be with me. Won't you?'

'Of course,' he says. 'All the way. I'll be right beside you.'

And then he wraps his good arm around me and holds me tight and then a little tighter. And as the moon passes behind a cloud and the night closes in again, I lay my head on his chest and listen to the rise and fall of his breath. What good would the world be if he wasn't in it?

# THE HEALER

The day dawns hot and sticky and filled with biting insects. In the sunlight, Black Johnnie's face is the colour of candle wax. The men are still asleep and can't be woken. I search for Billy the Fiddle but he is gone. I must do something, but what? Our ship is barely seaworthy. And even if I wanted to sail somewhere else to try to find a surgeon, the rowboat has gone.

It is almost dark when the Billy the Fiddle rounds the bend in the rowboat. I have spent the day dipping a flannel in cool water, trying to keep the captain's mouth moist and his head cool. He can't keep anything down any more. I am relieved to see Billy but, despite my hopes, he has not brought a surgeon. A young Indian girl climbs out of the dinghy and

151

follows him along the jetty. I am so furious I that I start to yell at him. How can he think of chasing women at a time like this? How could he forget Black Johnnie?

He has to hold me back with one huge arm or I would punch him.

'Silas, my boy,' he says softly, once he has got my arm in his vice-like grip. 'I like a woman as much any other, but this isn't what you think. This girl is a healer.'

I turn to look at her. She doesn't look like much of a healer to me. With her hair in braids and a necklace of animal teeth around her neck, she's surely only a few years older than I am.

'Then where are her medicines?' I demand.

'She uses plants,' he explains. 'She will gather what she needs.'

The girl stares as if she can see right to the bottom of me.

'Stand aside and let her through,' he tells me.

Reluctantly, I let her pass.

The *Tenacity*'s surgeon had accidentally left behind a fragment of bullet in the captain's shoulder. Once the metal has been removed with a knife held in a flame to make it white hot, the Indian girl stitches up the wound with animal gut. Next, she covers it with a brew of leaves that she has stewed in a pot for an hour. When she has wrapped the captain's arm and shoulder up in a piece of clean cloth, she gives him a draught and he falls asleep.

When he wakes hours later, the colour has returned to his cheeks. The girl changes the dressing and brews up another special potion. Clearly I was wrong about her. On the third day he is fit enough to take a walk around Skull Creek and drink a little French wine. But once he is out of danger, a gloom seems to descend on him. I feel it too, the swamp pressing down on me like a headache.

'How can I pay her?' he asks Billy the Fiddle. 'I have no money.'

'She has been paid,' he replies. 'Now, let's not hear any more about it.'

That evening, the girl is taken home, another pig is roasted and the pyrates' carousing goes on long into the night. Judging by the empty crates, Skull Creek's supplies of French wine and Jamaican rum must be almost gone.

'We are being shown so much generosity,' the captain says. 'It worries me.'

Once again, Billy the Fiddle shrugs and explains that we owe nothing.

Suddenly the captain's face pales once more.

'Bill, you haven't given me up, have you?'

Billy the Fiddle's face turns dark red. He is almost speechless with rage.

'What do you take me for?' he says. 'I am no turncoat, but an honourable man. In some respects, at least.'

'I'm sorry, it's just this place,' the captain explains. 'And once I have recovered, we still have the problem of what to do about the ship.'

Billy looks away but I catch a twinkle in his eye. There is something he's not telling us, I'm sure of it.

The next day, I am woken by a cry from the lagoon.

'Scarlet pantaloons,' a man's voice shouts.

'Come ashore!' booms Billy the Fiddle's voice in reply.

'We have only been here for a few days,' the captain says to me. 'And our Bill has the run of the place.'

A barge arrives, crewed by three rough-looking men and a small grey monkey. It is loaded up so high with goods and floats so low in the water that one large wave would sink it. We stand aside as the men start to unload the cargo. One by one, boxes of provisions including two crates of rum, three stacks of folded sailcloth and six coils of fresh rope are piled up on a sheet of brand new tarpaulin on the banks of the lagoon.

'We could be doing with some of this,' the captain says enviously. 'Who's it for?'

He looks around the shore as if another ship and its crew might just materialise from nowhere.

'For?' Billy the Fiddle replies. 'It's for us, of course. It's for the good ship, *Curby Dodger*.'

Black Johnnie stares at him for a moment in disbelief.

'But how?' he asks. 'How on earth did you find the money for all this, Bill?'

'Never look a gift horse in the mouth,' he says mysteriously. 'But I have my ways.'

The captain is lost in thought for a moment.

'You sold the advance guarantee!' he says.

'Not sold,' Billy corrects, 'pawned.' He pulls a small paper ticket from his waistcoat. 'When we're richer men and come through this way again we can buy it back.'

'But the crew?' the captain asks. 'The stone was for all of you.'

'The crew agreed,' Billy replies. 'There was a consensus. They didn't want to lose you. Or the reward.'

Black Johnnie blinks and I see a tear glisten in his eye. But he clears his throat and orders Billy the Fiddle to assemble the men. In the harsh light of day, it's obvious that the drinking and carousing have taken their toll. Most of them look much the worse for wear. Any longer in Skull Creek, with its suffocating climate and large reserves of booze, and who knows what kind of state they'd be in.

'We have no more time to waste,' the captain tells them. 'We shall be shipshape by dusk and I aim to catch the first tide tomorrow. You are free to stay here, to take your chances on the mainland. Or you are free to join me once more and continue on to our destination, the fair land of my birth, Scotland, where our mission concludes.'

'I have no mistress but the sea,' says one man. 'And I'm beginning to miss her.'

'Aye, aye,' chorus the others.

Black Johnnie's face breaks into a wide smile.

'Well that's just fine and dandy,' he says. 'Dandy and fine.'

# THE GREAT CIRCULAR

With the brand new sails and ropes made from finest manila hemp we set forth again, and, after navigating our way through the strung-out archipelago of the Florida Keys, we are soon back on course. Once or twice we spot a galleon or merchant ship in the far, far distance but since we are small, and partly camouflaged by the coast, they don't see us.

Just to the north of the Carolinas, by Billy the Fiddle's calculations, we hit a bank of thick fog. We sail on past New York, Provincetown at the tip of Cape Cod, Boston and then up towards Halifax, Nova Scotia. Like the captain, I spend hours peering out in the directions of these towns and settlements, desperate for a glimpse of them. But even though my eyes begin to ache, I still can't see more than a stone's throw from my toes. It is like being wrapped up in cotton wool. Only the change in temperature reveals that we are moving north at all.

It gets colder every day and by the time we're nearing Halifax we realise that we shall need more clothes if we don't want to freeze to death. According to Bill we should be almost there but we still can't see a thing.

'Are you sure?' asks the captain.

'Quite sure,' Billy the Fiddle replies. 'We should be entering the harbour about now.'

All at once some masts loom out of the fog. And beyond that Citadel Hill appears. We have arrived.

'Good work, Bill,' says the captain.

Once we have dropped the anchor and raised colours least likely to attract attention (an Irish flag that one of the pyrates stole from the first ship he plundered) Black Johnnie and several men head to shore. Halifax has many small trading posts and the captain comes back laden with seal-and-bear-skin jerkins, mittens and boots, plus a sack of beaver-fur hats that are all the rage, so they tell us, in London. The crew try everything on and there is much rejoicing until they discover that most of the boat's supply of rum has gone. The captain has exchanged it for warm clothes.

'I may have been cold,' one pyrate laments, 'but at least I was merry.'

The furs are too big and cumbersome for me. Even the hats fall down over my eyes and make everyone laugh.

'Here,' says the captain. 'This is yours.'

He hands me a bundle of soft white fur. As it unrolls in my arms it becomes a coat.

'It's made of polar bear,' he explains, 'stitched for a bride who never arrived.'

I almost drop it. I don't want to wear a dead person's clothes.

'Did she drown?' I ask.

'No,' he laughs. 'She just changed her mind. I thought it might be around your size. Does it fit?'

I pull it on around my shoulders. It falls right down to my knees. For the first time since we left Skull Creek, I feel warm.

'I never want to take it off,' I reply.

Off the coast of Newfoundland, the sea is full of herring and lobster. Although we have no more money for supplies, our nets and traps fill up. We sail the westerly trade, which will speed us steadily across the Atlantic. What lies ahead still keeps me awake at night.

Most nights are broken anyway. We all take turns on watch, four hours at a stretch, to look out for other vessels and icebergs. On the second day after leaving Newfoundland I spot an iceberg slowly approaching. It has two towering spires and its surface is a strange shade of blue. One of the pyrates decides to claim it as his own and so, even though everyone tells him it's far too dangerous, he takes the rowboat, rows across, climbs it and sticks a red neckerchief on a stick as a flag on the summit. He is known as Iceberg Jack from then on, a name he seems to like.

Other icebergs float serenely by, flat icebergs, spiked icebergs and icebergs with clefts or carved with caves. They are usually white but occasionally they are blue or blue creased with grey. Some of them are covered in nesting birds, others look as desolate as if they had come from the ends of the earth. Which, in fact, they have.

One early morning, the captain rouses me from the depths of sleep to join him on the deck. I pull my polar bear coat on and start my watch as the dawn begins to break. As usual, the colours of the rising sun dissolve in the fog, turning it pale gold and copper and the softest violet. When a bloom of white appears out of the mist on the starboard side at first I assume that it is just another iceberg. And then I hear the eerie sound of whistling. Before I can raise the alarm, a huge ship with three masts, a dozen sails and at least sixty guns, rears out of the fog. It flies the Spanish flag. I turn to look for the captain but he is already right beside me.

'Sssh,' he says, holding his finger to his lips.

We slip by so close that I can almost see right through the portholes. There is no one aboard. As we pass by I can see what I couldn't see before. The great ship is listing to one side with a huge hole ripped in its side.

'It must have hit a growler,' Black Johnnie says when we are out of earshot.

'What's a growler?' I ask.

'An iceberg that floats just beneath the surface of the sea,' he replies.

'So how can you spot one?' I ask.

'You can't,' he says.

'And where are all the crew?'

He shrugs. The fog clears a little and we look at out the rolling ocean.

'They could be anywhere,' he says.

A day later we come upon a wooden dinghy floating upside down in the sea.

'Oh, dear,' says Black Johnnie.

I try not to think about the drowned Spaniards or the threat of growlers as we sail on. Days turn into weeks and still there is no sight of Scotland. Even Billy the Fiddle starts to worry.

'If only we could see,' he says, 'then I would feel a whole lot better.'

And then one day the fog clears and there is land on either side, close, much closer, than any of us expected. I recognise the place immediately.

'By my calculations,' Billy the Fiddle tells us, 'we should be heading up the Firth of Clyde.'

Up ahead, two ancient castles – one on an island and one on the mainland – look like sentinels guarding the mouth of the river. We cannot pass by without being seen. The Irish flag is still flying. Billy the Fiddle glances at Black Johnnie. If he wants to change his mind, if he feels now that our mission is too dangerous – that it might be better to steal the Jewels of Caracas from Isabella, forfeit our reward and squander any possibility that she be reunited with her long-lost lover, then this would be the place to decide.

Black Johnnie rubs his shoulder and then he nods.

'Keep going, Bill,' he says. 'We've a fair wind behind us. We'll be in Glasgow by nightfall.'

# THE FAIR SHORES

Greenock, at the mouth of the Clyde, is far from being the huge, dirty, smelly town of my memory. From the ship I can see the harbour, the sugar warehouses, the tannery and, on the hill behind, the brewery and the parish school where I used to go. With its bright green fields and a fresh wind to blow away the smoke from its chimneys, the town is not the sad place I remembered. Maybe it isn't Greenock that has changed, but me?

I can barely picture my sister's face any more. It has been more than two years since we last saw each other. Is she still working as a housemaid? What did she think of me when I left without a word of farewell? Was she somehow involved in the attempt to bring me home? And if so, was she told I had drowned?

I am filled with a longing to see her again, to let her know that I tried my best, to tell her that soon, as soon as I can, I will send her enough money to let her start a new, better life. But that will have to wait. There is a price on the head of Jon Harkin. I know he risks much by coming here. Before we do anything else, we must fulfil my promise to James: deliver the jewels to William Dunlop and collect our reward.

The river grows narrower. Up ahead, built on a plug of volcanic rock, sits Dumbarton Castle. Although the wind has dropped, Black Johnnie shivers as we pass it.

'Are you cold?' I ask. 'Shall I fetch your coat?'

'No,' he says. 'I am fine. I have spent too long in the tropics. I am not used to the chill of the Scottish climate.'

I know how he feels. I pull my fur coat a little tighter around my shoulders but still the damp air seems to seep into my bones.

Just beyond Dumbarton we must anchor and transfer to a barge. The Clyde river is not deep enough for ships beyond this point.

'We'll be back tomorrow,' the captain tells the crew who volunteer to stay with the *Curby Dodger*. 'Try not to draw attention to yourselves.' It seems that the captain is not the only one who takes a risk by stepping on to Scottish soil.

Looking back, among the cutters and the three-mast sloops, the brigs and the snows, our ship doesn't stand out. After the long voyage her sails are tattered and her paintwork is peeling and crusty with salt spray. But, in spite of being a tub, she has got us across the Atlantic, through treacherous seas and thick, suffocating fog. And for that, despite her looks, I am ridiculously proud of her.

Although Glasgow is only twenty miles from Greenock, I have never been to the city before. I grew up hearing about it – about the thieves and cut-throats who hung around the Gallowgate Port and Skinner's Green, the university students of Rottenrow and the wealthy tobacco lords who, after making their fortune in the Colonies, parade along Goosedubs and the Saltmarket with their red capes and gold-tipped canes, looking over the city as if they own it. Which now, as I understand, they do.

It is evening by the time we approach Glasgow Bridge, with the Merchants' Steeple and the University Clock tower beyond. The rain is torrential. Even the polar bear coat is no match for Scottish weather and it is soaked in minutes.

'Shall we go to Dunlop now?' I ask.

The captain shakes his head.

'Respectable men do not receive visitors after

nightfall,' he says. 'Tomorrow shall suffice. Tonight we shall explore a little.'

While Billy the Fiddle spruces himself up to go looking for wine and women and song in any, he tells me, combination, the captain takes off his furs and his fine clothes, and buys a set of breeches and a jacket from one of the crew of the barge. Filthy, tatty and just a little too small, the clothes transform him. But if you look closely, you can tell by the way he holds his head and the spark in his eye that he is more than he first appears. And so he experiments with hats and eye-patches and even contemplates a limp.

'No one must know me,' he explains. 'You must not call me Black Johnnie but by another name.'

'What do you suggest?' I ask.

'How about something Irish?'

And so my captain, at least for our time in Scotland, becomes 'Paddy Kelly', an Irish importer of furs from Newfoundland.

'Do we know where Dunlop lives?' I ask.

'It can't be hard to find out,' he replies. 'Wealth has a habit of announcing itself to the world. I'm sure if we ask anyone, they'll know.'

# BONNIE PRINCE CHARLIE

The rain has stopped by the time we go ashore. Even at night, the Clyde is busy. As well as unloading tobacco and sugar by lamplight, the longshoremen are loading up several barges with cast-iron chains, guns, cotton, wool and linen. The chains and guns will be exchanged for captured Africans, the captain tells me, the linen woven into cloth and made into clothes for the slaves to wear on the plantations. Slaves' clothes made out of material usually used for sacks are one of Scotland's biggest exports.

'Everyone else makes a profit,' he points out. 'While the men and women who live and die on the plantations are paid nothing.'

Likewise, as we walk along Virginia Street and pass

the fine new houses of the tobacco merchants, the captain finds it hard to mask his disgust.

'Their palaces are not made of brick,' he says. 'But with the bones of dead men.'

We walk along the river and end up at a large stretch of land called Glasgow Green. It could not be a more peaceful place. And yet, the captain still looks troubled.

'It seems smaller than I remember it,' he says.

'You know it?' I ask.

'I was here before, in '45,' he says.

'You were here with the Jacobite army?'

'I was,' he says. 'It was just after Christmas.'

He pauses. But he's itching to tell me. It's obvious.

'Go on,' I say.

'I was here for ten days,' he says. 'The Green was all covered in snow. We tried to hoist up our temporary shelters but the ground was so hard with frost that it was almost impossible to hammer the stakes into the earth. We cut down a few trees and lit a fire but the men were still cold. No wonder. We'd marched all the way from Carlisle, and Derby before that. Our clothes had been soaked by the snow, dried by the heat of our own bodies and then, only an hour or two later, been soaked through all over again by more snow. Our skin was red raw from the wind and our boots worn right through at the soles. We didn't look like an army fighting for the restoration of the Stuarts to the throne, but a ragtaggle bunch of scallywags.'

At the brewery I remember my adoptive parents talking about Prince Charlie's army, calling them looters and plunders, thieves and cowards.

'I heard you held the city of Glasgow to ransom?' I say.

'We didn't ask for money,' he replies. 'Just food and supplies; for clothes, shirts, jackets and warm pairs of socks.'

'And you got them?'

He smiles and nods his head.

'Mostly,' he says. 'Plus flowers and sweet cakes and baskets of apples. Although many of the men of this city were loath to support him, the Young Pretender, Prince Charlie, was bonnie indeed. We had plenty of supporters here, women and girls who dressed up to the nines and came down when they heard that he was going to spend a few days here.'

'He was right here?' I ask. 'Bonnie Prince Charlie was here?'

He pauses and stares out at the green.

'Yes, he was,' he says. 'He stayed in Shawfield Mansion for most of the time. But he came down to the Green to raise morale and meet the men. You see it wasn't just women he had an effect on. I remember watching him walk from that tree, right there, down to the Clyde with all the men cheering and clapping and singing. And even though they'd marched for so long, and even though they'd fought at Derby and Carlisle and lost, and even though they were retreating rather than advancing, they still had faith in him.'

He blinks and I notice his eyes are wet.

'Of course, we won at Linlithgow,' he says and wipes his face with his sleeve. 'But we kept on being ordered to retreat, to Inverness, and then finally to Culloden in the north. Although we had been six thousand strong when we marched south, by that time we were fewer. And then we lost two thousand men on the moors.'

I stare down at my feet. I know what happened up there on Culloden Moor. The Jacobites, it was said, fought bravely but were butchered by the Duke of Cumberland and his men, who had pursued them from England like hounds after a fox.

'Afterwards everyone who was left alive turned and fled,' he says softly, 'throwing down their weapons, their worn-out boots, their drums and pipes as they ran. And still they kept on firing. My horse was hit and we both fell into a ditch. As I climbed out I came face to face with a redcoat with a sword in his hand.

He looked at me and I looked at him. I could see the fear in his eyes. I had blood on my clothes, my horse's blood, and a pistol in my hand, so he just lashed out. He caught me right in the belly.'

He runs his hand across his middle, the place where I have seen the white slice of a scar.

'At first I thought he'd got me,' he goes on. 'I lay there and waited to die. But it didn't happen. When night fell, I crawled through heather and mud and mire until I was far away enough away not to be seen. Slowly I made my way in the direction of the west coast.'

And then he falls silent. The clouds are racing through the sky above, throwing down rain one moment and letting rays of sun through the next.

'So what happened?' I insist. 'You reached the Clyde? You boarded a ship to the Colonies? What?'

He shakes his head.

'No,' he says. 'My wound wasn't serious but I was still bleeding. I would have died but for...' Here, he hesitates and looks at me.

'But for what?'

'A very kind person took me in,' he says.

'Let me guess,' I reply, 'a lady.'

'Yes,' he says, 'a lady.'

And here he smiles.

'Soon I would have been well enough to travel but

unfortunately, not soon enough. Her husband returned from business here in Glasgow unexpectedly and handed me in.'

'You were captured?'

'I was,' he replies. 'I was held at Dumbarton Castle. The lady came to see me every week and brought me food. She was very kind.'

'For how long?'

'Twelve months,' he says.

No wonder he had shivered as we passed Dumbarton on the Clyde.

'And then you escaped?' I ask. 'You were released? What happened? Tell me!'

He shakes his head and stares into the distance. 'Unfortunately not. I was taken to Liverpool along with 150 other Jacobites, where a judge ordered us to be exiled to the Colonies. We were to become indentured slaves.'

'You?' I say. 'A slave?'

Here his eyes flash.

'The only difference between me and the slaves who work in the Colonies is the colour of my skin.'

'I know,' I reply. 'I just couldn't imagine it. That's all.'

And then he sighs.

'I'm sorry. You see, I still can't understand how it could have changed so quickly. The Jacobites were winning. We believed we were going to put Charlie back where he belonged, on the throne. And even when we rested here, we thought we were winning. We believed that we would take Stirling, then Perth and then drop back and take Edinburgh again. In only a matter of months, however, dozens of my men, my friends, my leaders were caught and captured. Most of them are dead now.'

For a moment he is silent. And I think about the men who ate sweet cakes and pulled on brand new jackets and shirts for the march ahead, not knowing that in barely four months time they would die on the lonely, desolate moors of Culloden or end up strung from the gallows.

'So how did you escape?' I ask. 'Were you ever a slave?'

He turns to me and for a moment he looks as if he has forgotten who I am, as if in his head he is back in '45.

'We never reached the Americas,' he says. 'Our boat was captured by a French privateer who released us from our shackles and took us to France. It was from there as a free man that I sailed to the Colonies and took up the life of a buccaneer. I wasn't the only one, either. But that, as they say, is another story.'

A man is approaching on foot from the direction

of the city, a man in a black coat and hat with a silver-tipped cane in his hand. He pauses when he sees us.

'It is not permitted to loiter,' he says in a voice so loud he must presume we are both deaf. 'Take your son, my good man, and be off with you. This is a respectable neighbourhood.'

I turn to Black Johnnie, expecting him to give the man with the cane a cutting reply. But instead he simply bows his head and takes my hand.

'We have work to do,' he says, in a broad Irish accent. 'Come on, son.'

The man watches as we go and mutters something under his breath.

'Convincing?' the captain whispers.

'Very,' I reply.

# A WINK

I doze fitfully on the barge that night. The river is too calm. The air is too quiet. I get up at dawn. It is when I am staring out at the green fields and rough ground beyond the city that I notice a new barge has arrived during the night. A-ha! On it I spy Bart and Red Will and others from the *Tenacity* crew. They look as if they are shackled.

The captain is not happy about being woken up. But when I tell him what I have seen he leaps out of his bunk.

'My ship,' he says. 'My darling vessel. It must be anchored right now at Dumbarton, somewhere by the *Curby Dodger*.'

'So what shall we do?' I ask.

'Nothing,' he says. 'Nothing for now. One thing at a time. We deliver the jewels, Silas, just as you promised, but that is all. We'll get our ship back. Far from the eyes of magistrates and the like, we'll get her back.'

Everyone knows William Dunlop. He has built a house on a plot of land on Virginia Street that is so new that the paint is still drying on the walls. Some workmen are climbing up ropes to a wooden platform on the roof, while two more are painstakingly carving the stonework above the windows.

The captain has his hand on the bell and is just about to ring it when a butler throws open the front door. He jumps, visibly, when he sees us.

'Downstairs,' he says. 'Go round the back and you'll see the steps. Tell cook that the butler sent you, if it's food you're looking for.'

We stand aside and see the butler usher out William Dunlop. Dunlop has fair hair and grey eyes, the colour of rain. He is handsome, I suppose, and much younger than I had assumed. As he strides past us down the stone steps to meet a groom with a horse, my nose tickles with his cologne. He pulls himself up, tells his groom he'll be back in at noon and sets off down the street at a gallop.

So we have a couple of hours to wait, but time passes quickly in Glasgow. I wonder whether we should keep an eye out for McGregor and stay out of sight, avoiding the authorities, but the city is large and there is so much to see. On the wide streets there are theatres, coffee houses and private clubs, where ladies and gentlemen in powdered wigs drink tea and eat tiny cakes. In the market the stalls are piled high with fruit and vegetables, jugs of ale and loaves of bread, while grocers sell oranges and figs, tea from China and wine from France.

'Isn't it glorious?' I say.

The captain nods.

'For those who can afford it,' he says.

Just off the main streets is the clatter of a dozen factories or more: ropeworks, tobacco spinners, printers and dye manufacturers. Women sit at looms and weave flax to make linen cloth, while men twist vast spools of hemp or stir huge vats of scarlet dye made from crushed insects or bulls' blood. Children, my age and younger, carry vast baskets of coal on the their backs from the river to the factories or deliver goods from one place to another, their bodies bent double from the weight.

Although the pavements, like the streets, are unpaved, there is a single stretch that is laid with stone. It runs all the way from Glasgow Cross to a statue of King Billy. But when we walk on it, we are immediately ordered to get off. It is, we discover, only for the tobacco lords. Why? Because they paid for it. Everyone else, ladies, children and working men, have to walk to the side.

It is as we tramp through the thick brown mud that we come face to face with a middle-aged couple, who, not being rich or in the right business, also have to stay off the stone pavement. The woman has a pretty, unhappy face. The man is fat with eyes so deeply stuck in his face that he probably doesn't see anything but the space directly in front of his bulbous nose. As soon as she spots us, however, the lady stops dead.

'Jon,' she gasps. 'You're alive?' Then she covers her mouth with her hand.

I look up in an alarm at the captain's face. It doesn't change. He pretends he hasn't heard her.

'Excuse me, Madam, Sir,' he says and steps aside so they can pass.

As they walk on, the woman throws a quick glance back over her shoulder and gives Black Johnnie the hint of a smile. As I watch he gives her a wink in return. But his timing is bad and her husband, with a twist of his huge head, catches it.

'Oh, dear,' the captain says under his breath as we walk quickly away.

'Who was that?' I ask.

'An old friend,' he replies. 'One who deserves more than the life she has been dealt.'

'Was that her?' I ask. 'The one who nursed you after you were hurt at Culloden?'

'I was just thinking of her, and lo and behold, there she was! Her husband has handed me in once before. I have no doubt that he will do it again. We must make haste.'

# TWICE
# INTERRUPTED

For the second time that day we are on William Dunlop's doorstep. Black Johnnie stands to his full height. The Irish accent has gone.

'Tell your master we need to see him on a matter of some urgency,' he instructs the maid.

'The master is in his study,' she says, 'and cannot be disturbed.'

'You must disturb him,' he says. 'I will take the blame.' And then he gives the maid his most charming smile. She blushes.

'You had better come in then,' she says.

'Are we the first visitors today?' he asks, as she leads us up a set of shallow stairs to the first floor.

'No,' the maid says over her shoulder. 'There was a

sea captain who called early. He, too, had an urgent matter he wanted to discuss on his barge. My master has just returned from the meeting. Most upset he was'

'McGregor,' says Black Johnnie under his breath.

The room she shows us into is as wide as the house and grandly furnished. A crystal chandelier hangs from the ceiling and a roaring fire burns in the grate.

After a couple of minutes, William Dunlop strides into the room. He pauses before he speaks.

'My maid tells me that you want to see me about an urgent matter,' he says.

Black Johnnie turns and bows.

'Pleased to make your acquaintance,' he says.

There is a moment when the two men stare at each other, neither one stepping forward to greet the other.

'Have we met before?' Dunlop asks.

'You look familiar,' the captain agrees. 'Were you at Culloden?'

Dunlop shakes his head.

'It will come to me,' Black Johnnie laughs. 'I never forget a face.'

'So?' Dunlop asks. 'What can I do for you? My schooners and brigs are the best in Scotland, maybe the fastest this side of the Atlantic, but my customers are not normally quite so impatient.'

'We come from the other,' the captain says, 'side of the Atlantic.'

'We bring a shipment from Jamaica,' I continue.

Dunlop squints at me, on the brink of words. Before he can speak, I pull the brass tin from the waistband of my breeches then hand it over.

'It's from a lady by the name of Isabella.'

Dunlop looks at the tin in his hands for a moment before, carefully, he lifts the lid a fraction.

'It isn't locked?' he asks.

'It was,' I assure him. 'She packed the contents in a lead box, which James, her son, gave to me for safekeeping. I swapped it over. It's a long story.'

'Well, open it,' says Black Johnnie impatiently.

Dunlop throws back the lid. The Jewels of Caracas sparkle in the morning light: red and amber, aquamarine and pale sea green. For a moment no one says anything.

'I've found them,' Dunlop says. 'This morning, when the lock was forced, and the lead box was opened, I thought that all was lost.'

I catch the captain's eye. Is this the right answer?

'My wife and child,' he continues and his eyes blink with liquid. 'Thank you.'

Black Johnnie sighs with relief and then he looks, and looks again, at Dunlop.

'Wait a minute,' he says. 'We *have* met before.'

'That's right. Hello, Johnnie, we shared a cell...'

'Don't remind me,' the captain interrupts. 'Avery Blue, well, well, you've changed.'

'For the better?'

'That remains to be seen.'

'I've diversified,' he explains. 'My life changed ten years ago. You see, I misplaced my wife. She was carrying our child. I returned from my travels and found her gone. I know she thought me drowned. My letters were returned, my calls to her father's house refused. And I realised that it didn't matter how many ships we raided, how many jewels and coins I added to my stash, my greatest treasures were lost to me. And so I decided to leave the high seas and plough all my ill-gotten wealth into a respectable business.'

'You've done well,' the captain says.

'Thank you,' he replies. 'I searched for her. From the salons of London to the farthest reaches of the Colonies. Eventually I heard about a widow in Jamaica of the same name with a child of around ten. But how could either of us establish our identity without giving ourselves away or being taken for a ride by fortune hunters?'

'She sent you the Jewels of Caracas,' I say.

'So it seems,' he replies, picking up a handful of gems and dropping them again one by one. 'It's been a long while since I've seen these beauties.'

The clock strikes the hour. Black Johnnie clears his throat. We have no time, no time to lose.

'Well, that's that,' he says. 'You can claim your bride. And as for us?'

'Your reward,' he replies. 'Of course.'

Dunlop places the brass tin and its lid on a small wooden table in the centre of the room and pulls a bag of gold coins from high up in the chimney.

'What did she promise you? One hundred?'

He counts them out in tens but then hesitates.

'What would you say if I suggested an increase? How about I double the amount?' he continues. 'Two hundred gold coins. If...'

Black Johnnie's eyes widen further.

'If?'

'If you deliver an item to Isabella in return,'

He pulls a scarlet handkerchief from his pocket and hands it to the captain. It looks ordinary apart from two initials embroidered beautifully in one corner. The captain hands it to me for safekeeping.

'She will know it when she sees it,' Dunlop says. 'After all, she made it. I will pay you the full amount on completion of the task.'

'But we cannot come back here and claim it.'

'Sail as soon as you can. I have a few things to clear up here in Glasgow but I won't be far behind you. We'll pay you in full when I reach Kingston. Until then, take a gold piece for every member of your crew.'

He hands over the bag of coins and the two men shake on the deal.

There is a sharp knock on the door.

'Sir?' a woman's voice cries.

'Not now!' Dunlop calls back.

But the door opens anyway and the maid is pushed in and aside, revealing McGregor with his dirk drawn. Behind him are three more seamen, all armed.

'I thought our business was concluded,' Dunlop says.

'Not quite. You know who this man is?'

'Why?' he asks. 'Are you going to tell me?'

'He plundered my ship, then torched it!'

'It was your crew...' Black Johnnie begins.

'Not a word.' McGregor waves the knife towards the captain. And then his eyes fall on the open brass tin and the jewels.

'So why have you come?' Dunlop asks.

'Entertaining pyrates?' he replies. 'I'm sure the magistrates would be interested.'

'I paid you handsomely for your delivery, McGregor, despite it being an empty box, because I believed you brought it in good faith.' Dunlop's voice is low and hard. 'And now you wish to blackmail me?'

'It was empty?' says Black Johnnie. 'I see a better solution,' McGregor replies and then he nods to his men. 'Take that tin!' One of them picks it up, closes the lid then hands it over. 'Nice doing business with you.' McGregor nods as he pockets it.

As soon as they back out the door, Johnnie starts formulating a plan.

'He will go straight to his barge,' he begins. 'We could cut him off –'

'Wait!' Dunlop's command is quiet but absolute.

We stop and listen to their boots on the stairs and the slam of the front door.

'But they took the jewels!' I cry out. 'The Jewels of Caracas!'

'Shall I call the magistrates?' asks the maid.

'Magistrates! Heavens, no,' Dunlop replies. 'Is anyone hurt?'

He seems wholly unperturbed. Just how rich is he? But once he has dismissed the maid, he explains. He gained the Jewels of Caracas in strange circumstances.

'I'll tell you that tale another day. They *are* beautiful. Exquisitely beautiful, but despite their name, they are not jewels. They are made of carefully cut and polished glass. McGregor may be able to pass one or two off to the uninformed, but as soon as he tries a real jeweller, he will learn the truth. They are worth very little.

Certainly far less than the reward you have earned. And now they have done their work. They have told me that my Isabella is there, waiting, in Jamaica...'

And then he stops and listens.

'Not more visitors?'

Raised voices come from below, loud and harsh and filled with the kind of command that is hard to refuse.

'We have information,' one of them shouts. 'About a traitor by the name of Jon Harkin.'

'No,' the poor maid is saying. 'There is no one of that name here. We have no need of magistrates.'

The captain's face turns white.

'I should never have returned. Too many people know me here. Alas, I have been forsaken!'

In two strides Dunlop is at the door. With a twist of his wrist, he locks it. The door handle spins round and round but the door doesn't open.

'Open up,' shout the magistrates. 'Or we'll break it down!'

'Just a minute!' calls Dunlop.

'Is there any other way out?' the captain whispers.

'The window,' says Dunlop. 'You could try the window?'

Black Johnnie rushes to the sill and looks down, then up. Two ropes for workmen still hang from the roof. With a yank, he pulls up the window sash and climbs out on to the ledge. He gives each rope a tug; they're secure.

'You have the handkerchief?' Dunlop checks.

'We have,' I tell him.

'Silas,' Black Johnnie cries. 'Quick as you can!'

We stand on the sill, a rope each.

'One more thing,' says the captain to Dunlop. 'Did I hear you correctly? Did you say the lead box was empty?'

'Completely.'

We leap just as the door flies open. The magistrates, three of them, alerted to the whereabouts of a former Jacobite by the husband of the woman who had once tended Black Johnnie's wounds, can only watch as we launch ourselves off the sill and shimmy down the rope to the street. We are on the ground and away before they can even manage to pull the whistles from their pockets and blow them.

# TIME AND TIDE

We have no time, no time to lose. We must sail on the next tide. As soon as we reach the quay, the captain signals to Billy the Fiddle to come over and fetch us.

'I completely forgot about your sister,' the captain says. 'You should go now if you want to see her. You have two or three hours before the tide turns.'

'But,' I begin, 'I don't know how to start.'

'Just kiss her,' he advises. 'Actions speak louder than words!' He misunderstands me. I mean that I have never been to the house where she was a servant and have no way of knowing whether she's still there. 'No later than three hours. You know we can't wait for you.'

'You won't?' I say.

He shakes his head.

'Too much at stake, I'm afraid,' he says gently. 'It's in the pyrate code. We have to act in the interest of the majority.'

'I'll do my best,' I say. 'But it may take longer.'

Black Johnnie's face falls.

'I understand,' he says. 'And if this is goodbye, I want you to know that you were the most excellent boy,' he says. 'Thank you for all you have done for me.'

It starts to rain, the drops making circular patterns on the surface of the river.

'It's not a bad place,' he says as he glances round at the grey buildings. 'Once you get used to it.'

For a second I am torn so completely, I ache from head to toe. I want to head off to the high seas, to take the handkerchief to the beautiful Isabella, and then claim our reward from Dunlop. I want to win back the *Tenacity* by stealth or force from McGregor. I want to be a pyrate's boy. But more than that, I need to see Agnes; I vowed that I would.

'Here is Dunlop's handkerchief,' I say. 'Don't lose it whatever you do.'

He stares at me for a second and something in his face softens. With a scrape of wood along the stone of the quay, Billy arrives.

'Good luck' the captain says. 'Are we ready, Bill? We have a new mission, one that promises to be handsomely paid.'

'We're shipshape.'

'How long before the tide turns?'

'High tide is at five,' he replies.

There is a blast from a whistle somewhere nearby.

Black Johnnie climbs quickly into the boat.

'We'll expect you,' he calls before they push off. 'Up until the last possible moment. And if we don't see you then, I'll see you in the next life!'

I nod, then turn and run and run until I am so far away that I can't hear the slap of the water on the bow or of the captain and Bill's voices as they pull away from the quay. Without the captain, the dark tenements and filthy streets of Glasgow seem full of people with murderers' faces and butchers' hands. What have I done?

I know the house where my sister worked was in Argyle Street but am not sure where that is. Heading uphill from the river I find myself in a cobbled street where the houses all have brass plates above their doorbells. As I walk, my eyes glance over engraved names and respectable professions: doctors and importers, bookkeepers and lawyers. When I see the sign on the last house, I stop in my tracks. It's a name that I know.

# CRAWFORD AND SWANN, SOLICITORS AND NOTARIES

And in my head I'm suddenly on the sinking ship five days out of Kingston again, with the lady who had been hired to take me away from my old life on Ferguson's plantation. I hear her voice as if she were standing right next to me. *Crawford and Swann.* I look back at the sign and read it once more.

An old man with long white whiskers and coal black eyes has come out of the office and looks as if he is about to head home at the end of the day.

'Can I help you?' he asks when he sees my expression.

'Perhaps,' I reply. 'If you are Mr Crawford?'

'Actually, I'm Mr Swann,' he replies. 'And you are?'

'I'm Silas Orr,' I say.

It takes a moment for the old man to place the name. But when he does, he nods.

'In that case,' he says. 'You had better come in. We have a lot to talk about.'

Once he has found the file and blown it free of dust he tells me that I am the sole inheritor of a linen mill in the town of Lanark.

'Your great-uncle left it to you in his will,' Mr Swann explains. 'Since we were unable to locate you it has been shut up for the last few years. But now you are back, I'm sure it wouldn't take much to get it running again. I am told, by those who know of such matters, that it has the potential to turn a tidy profit.'

'I don't understand,' I say.

'We did try to find you. We paid a respectable woman quite a large fee but she disappeared without...'

'Not that,' I interject. 'What great-uncle?'

The lawyer lifts his great dark eyes to look at me.

'Cuthbert Douglas,' he says. 'He was your father's mother's brother. Estranged, I am now given to understand. Well, if you will just sign a couple of papers. You are young, but I know there is no guardian to act on your behalf.'

I glance up at the clock. It is already almost three. I imagine the *Curby Dodger* straining at her anchor in the current. In two hours it will be high tide.

I sign once, twice, three times until finally the lawyer is satisfied. He hands me a copy of the deeds to the linen mill.

'Do with them what you will,' he tells me.

'What did my sister receive?' I ask.

He checks his papers.

'Nothing,' he says. 'It seems it all went to you – the closest living male relative. So what are your instructions? What am I to do?'

I have no idea what I should instruct and it must be obvious. He blinks twice and then shrugs.

'Would you like an advance?' he asks softly. 'Say, four silver coins? Just until you decide what steps to take next.'

'I don't want any debts,' I reply.

Mr Swann smiles.

'It is an advance of monies held in trust,' he explains. 'Master Orr, it is *your* money.'

How strange to find a life in the last place I had been expecting. My fortunes have changed in the blink of an eye. I don't have to risk my neck as a pyrate anymore. I am suddenly and unexpectedly established.

## AGNES

I knock on doors in Argyle Street and make enquiries but no one has heard of a servant girl called Agnes Orr. On the corner is a grocer's shop with a basket of lemons in the window. While the shop girl is serving someone, I pick one up and sniff. It reminds me of Agnes, of the lemons she used to bring me on her day off.

'Please don't handle the merchandise,' the shop girl tells me. 'If you're not going to buy anything then be off with you! I have to pay out of my own pocket for anything stolen.'

Despite all the delicious food stacked around her, the girl is thin and pale. She is allowed to sell the fruit and the figs, the nuts and the cakes, but not to eat them.

'I'm looking for Agnes Orr,' I say boldly as I put the lemon back.

'You are, are you?' she says, as she wraps up a piece of bacon.

'Do you know her?' I ask.

'Know her?' the girl laughs. 'Of course I know her.'

'Why do you laugh?' I ask, my heart lifting.

'Oh nothing,' she says. 'It's just that she always wants her daily delivery by three. And you should hear the fuss she makes if she doesn't get it.'

'But it is already well past three,' I point out.

She turns and looks at a large clock that hangs above.

'Glory be, so it is,' she says. 'Well, I'll be in for it again.'

A small boy sidles into the shop. He snatches an orange and makes off with it.

'Hey!' the girl shouts.

I am after the boy before he even noticed I was there. He may think he is quick but my time on the sea has made me nimble, and his twists and turns, his ducks and dives, are nothing compared to mine. I have him by the time we reach the next corner.

'Let go,' he yells, as I twist his arm.

'Give me back the orange!' I say.

He drops the fruit and it rolls into a puddle.

'Don't hand me in,' he whispers. 'It was for my ma. She isn't well. I've only left her to sell the horse in the market.'

Closer up, he looks much younger. His arm feels like a couple of bones in a sack. I let him go.

'Don't come back,' I tell him. 'If anyone else had caught you, you'd be in the clinker.'

A huge delivery of bread has just arrived and the shop girl is staring at it as if she wished she could make it disappear just by looking.

'I could do the delivery to Agnes Orr for you if you wanted,' I tell her as I hand her back the orange.

The girl shakes her head.

'I don't know you from Adam,' she says.

'I'm Agnes' brother,' I tell her. 'Been at sea for the last few years.'

The girl looks at me and then shakes her head.

'I do see a likeness. You should have told me that in the first place.'

The door opens and a whole gaggle of ladies crowd in and start picking up the fruit and squeezing it. The shop girl sighs and brings out a sealed box from beneath the counter. An address has been written on a piece of paper and attached to the top.

'It's just along a bit. You can't miss it. A nice place. Flowers outside.'

I find the house and knock twice. A maid takes the box from my hands.

'Better late than never,' she says.

'Is Agnes in?' I ask. 'I mean, would I be able to see her?'

'Who is it?' calls a voice from inside.

'Just the delivery boy, ma'am,' the maid answers.

'Ma'am?' I must have made a mistake. I'm about to make my excuses and run when a figure appears in the hallway. It is so dark that it takes me a moment to work out that it is a young woman.

'Silas!' the woman says. 'Silas? Is that you?'

Agnes holds me so hard that if I were a piece of crockery I would crack.

'It is you!' she says. 'My dear, dear sweet boy.'

I am waiting for someone to tell her to get back downstairs but that doesn't happen.

'I'll bring some tea, ma'am,' the maid tells Agnes. 'And cake.'

'Thank you,' Agnes says.

Agnes, my sister, is not a housemaid anymore. She leads me into a comfortable sitting room and bids me sit down near an old lady.

'This is my soon-to-be mother-in-law,' she explains, introducing us. 'I am engaged to be married.'

She tells me how shortly after I ran away, she met a

weaver at the market. They fell in love and he invited her to move in with his family and work with them. Money is a little tight but business is good.

My plan comes to me as she speaks. By the time she has finished telling me her story, I have the perfect solution.

'And what of you?' she asks. 'I heard you left the plantation. When I heard no news, I thought the worst.'

My story is long. I don't know where to start, and I have no time left.

'I am well,' I say. 'Very well in fact. And I can't tell you how glad I am that you are well too. But I must go.'

'You've only just arrived.'

I hand her the deeds to the mill and a couple of the silver coins.

'This is for you,' I say.

'What is it?'

'A present. From me and our Great-uncle Cuthbert Douglas.'

She frowns.

'Who?'

# AT A GALLOP

Even though I run all the way, I reach Greyfriar's Port just after the clock strikes five. I am too late. The barge is not there.

I sit down at the quayside with my head in my hands. What should I do now? Where should I go? How am I to catch my ship? A dozen men in a very light craft could row after them but by the time I could organise it, the tide would be against us.

I sob my heart out without caring who sees. I am marooned. All over again, I am lost. And then I hear the clatter of hooves and look up to see a face I recognise. It is the boy who stole the orange from the grocery shop, riding on the back of a beautiful black mare.

'Hey,' I call out.

He starts when he sees me and then looks around suspiciously. But there are no magistrates or shop owners.

'Nobody bought her?' I ask.

He shakes his head. And then I have an idea.

'I have a proposition,' I tell him. 'A way you can make an honest penny.'

As soon as he agrees, I clamber up behind him. And then we're off, riding, fast, much faster than the river's current, over the bridge and along the main bridle path. We overtake everyone in our way, streak past Dumbarton on the far bank, and reach Greenock in just over an hour.

I climb down and hand the boy my last pieces of silver.

'Take them. You can buy your mother a whole basket of oranges,' I tell him. 'And I won't need them where I'm going.'

I pull off my boots, tie the laces together and throw them around my neck. Then I grab a plank to keep me afloat, and step into the water.

'Where are you going?' he asks.

'Jamaica.'

Black Johnnie is standing on the deck, staring back along the ship's wake when I creep up behind him.

'Lost something?' I ask.

He spins round and even though I am soaking wet and exhausted from kicking in the cold current from the quay to the ship, he almost hugs all the breath out of me.

'I had lost a little bit of my heart,' he says. 'But it appears that it has now returned. How on earth did you get here?'

I tell him about the boy and his horse and how we rode all the way to Greenock.

'And your sister?' he asks.

'She is well,' I reply. 'Very well, in fact.'

We stand on the deck of the *Curby Dodger* and watch as the sea widens out and the land shrinks. Soon all that is left of Scotland are a few distant pricks of light.

# AN UNEXPECTED RE-ACQUAINTANCE

Our plan is to head due south towards the Azores Islands. If we catch the Gulf Stream it will carry us all the way to the Windward Islands in no time. We have the advantage, the captain tells me. From there, Jamaica is only a couple of days' sail, as long as the wind is behind us.

Once we have left Europe, the sea is so full of life that every morning the decks are covered in stranded flying fish that have landed there in the night. The crew are the happiest I've ever seen them, with good weather, easy sailing, Dunlop's gold pieces in their pockets, and the promise of more to come. Black Johnnie is also cheerful.

'Someone stole my stash from McGregor,' he says.

'That's good. That's very good. But who? And how? And where could it be now?'

It is nearly night when we reach the coast of Jamaica. The Blue Mountains, their slopes covered in dense green jungle, rise up into the distance. I can smell the familiar bitter scent of the coffee plantations above the sharp tang of the sea. Black Johnnie decides to head around to the north side of the island and so we drop anchor in a small, sheltered cove. Although it would be hard to spot the *Curby Dodger* from the open seas, we are clearly visible from the shore.

'We are only a few miles from Port Antonio,' Black Johnnie tells us, 'and the British garrison. I will row to the harbour and do some investigating. Once we know where Isabella's plantation is, we can make our delivery, claim our rewards and you'll be lying on the beach of your dreams by the coming of the spring tide.'

He raises a fist and shakes it in the air. I glance round at the men's faces. In the light of the moon I can see what they are thinking: white sand beneath their toes and a quart of rum by their side, a heavy purse in their pocket and a girl to wash their shirts and rub their backs. With the reward they are promised they could give up this life if they wished, and settle down on dry land. They would be freed from the possibility of enslavement or danger, poverty or sickness. No wonder they follow Black Johnnie so faithfully. Like me, they have nothing to lose and everything to gain. And yet, it must be said, a pyrate's life is unlike any other.

We watch the captain paddle off alone in the rowboat. He is wearing his disguise again and looks less like a pyrate captain and more like a tramp.

That night I am on watch. I admit I might have closed my eyes for a moment or two and so I didn't hear a single noise, not a splash of an oar or the glide of a hull on still water. The first thing I feel is the cold slash of steel pressed down on my neck and the poke of a knee in my belly.

'Move an inch and you die,' a girl's voice whispers in my ear.

I open my mouth to protest. The blade presses harder.

'You heard me,' the voice insists.

*Not again*, I tell myself. But I stay very, very still.

Somewhere on the island, a bell tolls. A cloud has covered the moon and there is barely any light to see by. I can just about make out that my captor wears a mask woven from banana leaves. All I can see is the dull glimmer of a pair of eyes.

'What is your cargo?' the voice whispers.

'We don't have any,' I reply.

'You have nothing?' the voice asks incredulously. 'So what have you come here for?'

As I try to formulate an answer, a movement catches my eye. My captor has not come alone. There are at least two dozen others ransacking the ship. While the crew sleeps on, one of them tips a sack of porridge oats over the side. Another slashes the ropes and then runs a knife through the mainsail methodically, as far as he can reach, ripping it almost in two. A third comes out of the captain's cabin with a velvet bag held above his head.

'Look what I found,' he squeals and starts to hop up and down.

I know the bag. It belongs to the captain and is full of small change. It is practically worthless. And then it strikes me that all of the mask-wearers are small. Their voices are high-pitched and their movements nimble. Children. There isn't, I'd guess, a single one older than me.

'You lied,' says my captor. 'Say your prayers. Or prepare to die!'

As the knife is drawn back to my ear to give good leverage, I tilt my head.

'Silas?' my captor's tone has changed completely. 'Is it really you?' She lowers the knife and lifts her mask.

'Catherine?' I whisper.

She examines my face as I examine hers. Her skin is tanned and her hair has been bleached by the sun, but the determined jut of her chin is unmistakeable. It is Catherine, my companion from the long first journey to Jamaica.

In the moment or two that it has taken for the two of us to recognise each other, the captain returns from Port Antonio.

'What on earth?' he shouts. 'Men wake up!'

One by one, the crew of the *Curby Dodger* tumble out on deck.

'Look what they have done to the sails,' the captain says. 'Grab hold of them!'

Billy the Fiddle has two of them by the hair. Black Johnnie dives after the boy with the small bag but he leaps over the side before the captain can stop him. Catherine jumps to her feet and holds her knife out in front of her, but she doesn't see the pyrate with the scar across his lip come creeping up behind her until the very last moment. And then she turns and screams and tries to get away. As he grabs her by the ankle, she turns around and bites him on the arm.

'Wait!' I yell, but my voice is not loud enough to cut through cries of pain and the shouts of fury. 'Stop!' I shout. But no one does.

And so I run to the captain and pull his musket

from his belt, hold it up in the air and fire. The blast deafens me. As the swirl of smoke disperses, I can see that everyone is staring at me.

'Stop!' I say. 'Everyone, stop, before someone gets hurt. They're only children!'

It takes a moment before the pyrates take in what I have said. And then they pull the masks from the intruders' faces. Black, white, yellow, the children are all races and range in age from about six to twelve.

'She bit me!' says the pyrate who has Catherine.

'You were hurting me!' she cries back.

They all start to argue about who hurt who when the captain raises his hand.

'But look what you did,' he says.

Everyone stops and takes a look at the state of the *Curby Dodger*. What is left of her sails flaps forlornly in the wind, while the severed ropes, the halyard and leach line, the boltrope and the painter lie in useless coils on the deck. Apart from the cost, it would take a week or more to fix her up again. And we all know we don't have that amount of time.

In the west I suddenly notice an orange glow in the air. A vessel is approaching around the headland. Like cockroaches when a light hits them, the children, including Catherine, scuttle over the sides and are gone.

'Quiet,' orders the captain. We are all silent as a huge

British warship appears in the distance brought, I now suspect, by my firing of the gun. Everyone is looking at Black Johnnie. But what can we do? We can't outrun them, not with our ship in this state. What choices does he have? And so he sighs, rubs his brow and then says the unthinkable.

'Grab your worldly goods and make for the shore,' he commands. 'And the last man off, open the scuppers.'

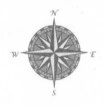

# THE WINDING
# PATH

There is no time to be shocked. I hurry below deck to my bunk, grab William Dunlop's handkerchief from the captain's cabin, a few clothes, my slingshot and pebbles and the silver-buckled shoes that the captain bought for me in Martinique, then rush back on deck. With so many belongings, there isn't enough space in the rowboat for us all and so some volunteer to swim, while the rest of us take an oar and prepare to row ashore.

It is one thing to open the scuppers to let in enough water to mop the decks, but quite another to open them and leave them open. Billy the Fiddle does the honours. As we wait for him to finish we sit in the bob of the rowboat and listen to the awful sound of water rushing into the hull. At first it is just a sigh, a low hiss like the escape of air through a hole. But then the sea seems to know it has our boat and the sigh turns into a rumble and the rumble into a roar, as gallons of water pour into the hold.

'Row fast, now,' whispers Bill as he climbs in to the dinghy beside us. 'Or she will bring us down with her.'

It only takes about five minutes for our ship to sink. By that time we are all standing on the shore with our hats in our hands.

'Goodbye, my good lady,' whispers Black Johnnie.

Her bow goes down first, the bowsprit spearing its way towards the murky sand of the ocean's bottom. The rigging tangles and snags as anything loose comes sliding down the decks before it is all sucked under and then, with a single bang of her tiller and the snapping of a mast, the *Curby Dodger* disappears, leaving nothing on the surface but a swirl of flat water and a short end of fraying rope.

From the cover of the trees along the shoreline we watch the British warship as it approaches along the coast towards us. It sails so close that we can see the faces of the sailors manning the cannons, and the captain who eyes the shore with his telescope. And then, as silently as it came, the ship glides around the tip of the bay and is gone.

'Think they will be back?' Billy the Fiddle asks out loud. No one replies. It doesn't seem to matter now.

There is nothing, as I have said before, as hopeless as a pyrate without a ship. Dry land feels too hard, too still, too rigid underfoot. Even sleep is impossible to men and boys so used to being rocked by the lull of the ocean. And so there is more than one man who wipes a tear from his eye at the scuppering of a ship that we had all once thought of as just a tub. She had survived a volcano's eruption and navigated icebergs and monumental storms. She was never beautiful or fast like the *Tenacity*, but we had loved her and hadn't realised it. And now she is gone.

'Do not despair,' says Black Johnnie, 'we are still to recover my own beautiful ship. Every man here shall have a place on her, should he wish it.'

He turns and surveys the jungle behind us.

'We had better get a move on,' he says. 'We have a delivery to make.' He turns and eyes the crew and makes a hasty decision. 'I found out that our reward can be found at a plantation is just on the other side of this mountain,' he tells us. 'But we can't all go. The rest of you can head to Kingston in shifts in the rowboat and wait for us. We shouldn't be more than a couple of days.'

Everyone agrees it is a reasonable plan.

We make camp there for the rest of the night, then head out in the morning. The mountainside is steep and the jungle is thick.

'Silas,' the captain asks, 'do you still have that compass I gave you?'

Of course I don't. I left it with most of my other belongings on the *Tenacity* in Martinique. But I don't want to let the captain down.

'I used to live in Jamaica,' I say. 'I don't need a compass. Follow me.'

Billy the Fiddle, carrying a large sack, and Black Johnnie follow me up a jungle path.

Of course, we get lost in a matter of hours. Soon I have no idea which way is up and which is down or if, indeed, we have been walking in circles. Eventually I find a clearing and come to a halt.

'Are we almost there?' the captain asks. 'How much further?'

'We must have walked for miles already,' adds Billy. 'I'm exhausted. Shall we stop and eat something or shall we wait until we arrive?'

How can I admit that I have no idea where we are?

'I'll check our bearings from over there,' I say, playing for time.

'I'll just take forty winks, then,' says Billy.

'I'll join you,' says the captain.

I walk to the top of a small hillock and try to look out. The jungle is even thicker here than it was on the coast. And then suddenly, a figure rises up right in front of me. I nearly jump out of my skin.

'Catherine!' I gasp. 'What are you doing here?'

'Following you,' she says. 'Your trail is quite erratic. You were at the exact same spot an hour ago.'

'I'm lost,' I tell her.

'Everyone gets lost the first time.' I stare at her as she sweeps her hair behind her ears. 'Is it really you, Silas Orr?' she asks. 'I heard you'd drowned.'

'Nearly did,' I say. 'But then I was saved. What about you?'

'I ran away,' she replies.

Quickly, we swap stories and she tells me how she escaped to the jungle rather than spend another six years held captive by her mean employer, how she met a bunch of other children and formed a camp in the jungle. In turn, I tell her of my ordeal at sea and how I met Black Johnnie and how he offered me a position.

'A pyrate's boy!' she gasps, her eyes wide. 'Is it wonderful?'

'It has its moments,' I shrug.

The sun above is beginning to drop. Without realising it, we have talked for a couple of hours.

From not far away, there is a low hoot followed by a series of three shorter ones. Catherine leaps to her feet.

'Soldiers,' she says. 'It's the sign, from the others.'

Her skin, so tanned by the sun, turns pale. She cocks her head and listens, and sure enough even I can hear the tramp of broken branches underfoot, the slash of a machete and the low murmur of men's voices.

'Wake your friends,' she says. 'Then follow me.'

Black Johnnie and Billy the Fiddle don't need much rousing. In a whisper, I explain the situation.

'Can we trust her?' asks the captain. 'After what she did?'

'I can vouch for her,' I say. 'Besides, what choice do we have?'

## THE
## ENCAMPMENT

Catherine knows the paths of the jungle, she knows where to cross the river and how to climb up a gully, she knows the short cuts and the long ways round that avoid the thickest tangles of undergrowth. At first she moves so fast that we can barely keep up with her, padding softly over the fallen leaves and carpet of moss at something between a run and a canter. Occasionally we lose her and she has to run back the way she has come to urge us to move faster. We seem at last to have left the soldiers behind.

'Not much further,' she promises. 'And then you can rest.'

At last, she lets us pause.

The path starts to lead back down the mountain

216

into a thicket of small shrubs and trees. A cliff rears up behind us. It looks impossibly high but there are creepers that you could use like rigging to scale the mast.

'I think there's a plantation a mile north of here,' she says.

'Why don't I go up there and take a look?' I ask. 'I'll be able to see everything.'

'If you're confident climbing that high,' she says. 'And if you're *quick*.'

The creepers twist down from stunted trees that grow in the cracks of the cliff. When one runs out there is usually another to grab on to but sometimes I have to edge a few feet along a small ledge or up a sheer rock face to reach it. Several times I get stuck and, with sweat dripping into my eyes and sheer panic in my chest, I make myself reach up, up as far as can until my fingers curl around the smallest indent. And then I flatten my whole body to the surface of rock and edge slow, slowly until my foot finds a niche in the cliff and I can hoist myself up and grab hold of another creeper.

Near the top, the creeper I am climbing thins to a few strands, not strong enough by any means to support me should I slip. And so my heart is beating wildly as I throw first one leg and then the next over the edge of the cliff-top, roll over, close my eyes and vow never to volunteer to do such a stupid thing again.

A shadow falls. I open my eyes. Three faces, blackened with mud, stare down at me. Three sharp wooden spears are aimed at my neck. Very slowly I sit up.

'What have you done with her?' one of them says.

'If you're looking for Catherine,' I say, 'she's a friend. She's just down there, actually.'

At that moment, however, I hear her scream. We all peer over the cliff edge. Down below, the captain, Bill and Catherine are surrounded by soldiers. One of them is pointing a musket at the captain's head.

'How did they find us?' I say.

'They have trackers,' the boy replies.

We lie low and watch as they are led along the path until they disappear into the jungle.

'Where are they going?' I ask.

The children shrug.

'We should follow them!' I insist.

'There's nothing we can do,' he tells me. 'There will be more soldiers following behind. You should come with us.'

And so, with the tip of a spear prodding into my back the entire way, I am pushed along a steep winding path that leads down the back of the cliff, through one stream then another, until we finally reach a clump of banyan trees and stop.

'We're here,' the boy says.

I suspect that they have deliberately led me round and round and up and down just to confuse me, so I am in a foul temper when I finally slump down in the shade of their so-called camp. It looks, in truth, like nothing much, just the clump of trees with a clearing in the middle. I wonder where they sleep? I wonder what they eat? A few smaller children stand a few feet away from me and stare. One of the ones who caught me sits down nearby and starts to fashion a new spear from a length of bamboo. He looks at me sidelong. His skin is white but his hair is jet black. He must be only a year or two younger than I am.

'You might need this,' he says. 'It gets cold at night.' And then he throws me an old ship's blanket. 'Where did you learn to scale a cliff?'

'I can climb a ship's rig,' I shrug. 'It's almost the same.'

'You been at sea for long?'

I think of the many voyages I have made, of storms and fair weather, of passing icebergs and lying stretched out on the bowsprit in the sun, and nod my head.

'A while,' I reply.

'I was sick all the way,' he tells me, 'when I came from Liverpool.'

'It is common,' I tell him. 'On my first voyage I was ill. But not as ill as Catherine was.'

The boy starts when I say her name.

'You know Catherine?' he asks.

'Didn't she explain? We both sailed from Greenock together bound for the plantations. It seems neither of us lasted long as an indentured servant.'

'So you weren't keeping her captive?' he asks.

'No!'

'Are you sure?'

I shake my head. He squints at me, as if wondering whether to believe it.

'Well,' he says finally, 'a friend of Catherine's is a friend of mine. Follow me.' And then he slots his foot into a crease in the trunk of the nearest banyan tree and hoists himself up.

From the bottom I can't see anything, just leaves and branches. But once I am about twenty feet off the ground, I push myself through a tiny hole and another world unfolds.

Although there is no floor, there are a series of wide branches that criss-cross back and forth to create a level. Two-dozen hammocks of varying sizes, woven from hemp, swing from branches, while bananas, mangoes and breadfruit hang in nets. There is even a small fire, with a pot suspended above it, constructed in the fork of a trunk. Its chimney is made from a tube of banana leaves and rises up above the tree canopy to take away the smell of smoke.

About twenty children sit clustered on a wide branch and wait for their supper to be cooked. They stand up in alarm when they see me.

'It's all right,' says the boy who led me up. 'He's a friend of Catherine's.'

'Where is Catherine?' one of them asks.

'The soldiers got her,' the boy says.

The children gasp. One starts to cry, which sets off another few.

'Where have they taken her?' another asks.

The boy shrugs.

'You know what we all agreed,' he says. 'No rescue attempts. If they find out where we are, then we're all goners.'

'But it's Catherine,' another sobs.

'It was her rule,' the boy replies.

Suddenly there is a hoot. Ash is thrown over the fire and the children all fall silent. I listen as hard as I can. At first I can't hear anything, just the wind in the branches above. And then I make out the soft fall of feet on the jungle floor. I look down. Right below us are three black tricorn hats: soldiers. One of them picks up the ship's blanket that I have left. He throws it over his shoulder. Just as well I'm up here and not down there any more.

I look over at the boy. He is staring at me, willing me not to make a sound. The soldiers are looking around, searching, I suppose, for the owner of the blanket. I tell myself that they can't see me. But I still can't stop trembling.

They stand there for what seems like ages and then slowly move off. They seem to know that they have missed something, they just don't know that it is twenty feet above their heads.

A few minutes later there is another hoot. The men have gone. Everyone relaxes. Using a flint, one of the children relights the fire. Once more they turn their attention to me.

'Isn't he too big?' a little child asks. 'How old are you?'

The question takes me by surprise. I don't know exactly. I haven't had a birthday since I left Scotland. Twelve, I tell them, or maybe thirteen.

'He came through the hole,' says the boy who brought me. 'He is not too big.'

And then he rubs his hand on his threadbare trousers and offers it.

'I'm Jonathan Lamont,' he offers.

'Silas Orr,' I reply.

'Oscar,' says another small boy and rises up to

shake my hand. One by one, the children introduce themselves, some with second names like Jonathan, and some without – forgotten, I suppose, or simply discarded along the way.

Some of the children, they tell me, absconded from the British Navy where they had been almost worked to death on ships as powder monkeys or cabin boys. Others, like Catherine, broke their bonds and escaped from cruel plantation owners. Those with black skins are the children of slaves, sent out into the jungle by their mothers rather than spend the rest of their life subjected to overwork and random cruel punishment.

'The soldiers won't keep your captain for long,' says Jonathan. 'Or the others.'

'What do you mean?' I ask.

'If they know there's a price on his head they'll take them all to Kingston.'

'Why Kingston?'

Oscar shrugs.

'That's where they take all the pyrates. And those associated with them. To Port Royal. They hang them at Gallows Point.'

My eyes well up, my ears start to roar and I struggle to keep my face straight. Never to see Black Johnnie again, or Billy the Fiddle, or Catherine is unbearable. I must help them. But how?

I decide I must go to Kingston and then to Port Royal. Immediately. Maybe in the future I will find Isabella and James, but right now I must rescue my dearest friends.

'How do you get there from here?' I ask.

'We'll show you, but we're not allowed to go to Kingston,' says Oscar. 'Too dangerous.'

'It's all right,' I tell him. 'I shall go alone.'

'You need to head north until you reach the waterfall,' Oscar says. 'Then take the path that leads down the hill. It's about three hours' walk to the bay. When you reach a paved road you'll know you're close. Take care.'

I thank them, take the supplies they offer, then slip through the hole, climb down the trunk and drop silently on to the forest floor. Even though I know they are watching me go, I can't see the children up above. I wave anyway and then, as they have told me to, I head north and walk for some time.

At the waterfall, I hear a giggle from a bush.

'I know you're in there,' I yell.

Around twenty children step out, each carrying a small pack of supplies.

'We know we're not supposed to,' one of them admits. 'But we want to come and rescue Catherine with you. Besides, you'd get lost without us. You've already taken the wrong turning twice.'

Oscar and Jonathan take the lead. It is just as well as the jungle is thick and I doubt whether I would have been able to find my way. It is dark by the time we reach the coast. The lights of the town spill out over the black water of the bay until they almost touch the collapsing towers and flooded alleyways of Port Royal. A flickering fire burns on Gallows Point. We build a makeshift camp just outside the town in a small clearing.

'So what's your plan?' one of the children asks me.

'I'm going to see what I can find out,' I tell them. 'If I'm not back by dawn, come and look for me. And if you can't find me, do something drastic!'

# THE CAPTIVE

The taverns on Harbour Street are all full tonight. Drunk men stagger out carrying bottles of rum. I slip into the nearest one. The air reeks of tobacco and sweat. The light is low and only a couple of candles flicker on the bar. I try to hold my breath and keep my head down. Nobody notices me, so I crouch in a corner and listen. There is, I soon gather, a ship with a cargo of slaves due to dock the next day. Many owners and managers have ridden down from the plantations to go to the sale. A hot summer, one tells another, has spread disease.

'Mine are dying like flies,' he says. 'And so one must keep topping up the stock.'

'I am in the same position,' says the other. 'The expense is eating into my profits.'

But most of the talk is of the hanging.

'A Jacobite!' says one woman with a large red nose. 'And a pyrate! Handsome too, I've heard.'

'Deserves to swing,' shouts a man with a sweaty face.

'Where is he being held?' another lady asks.

'It's a secret!'

'Go on?' the lady coaxes. 'You can tell me.'

He leans over to whisper in her ear. But he is so drunk and he has such a bellowing voice that the whole tavern can hear him without even trying.

'In Port Royal.'

I slip out of the tavern and head down to the harbour. The last time I was here, I was on my way back to Scotland. It scared me then. But that was before I met Black Johnnie, before I became a pyrate's boy. I pull myself up to my full height. I have survived storms at sea, I tell myself, I have almost drowned more than once. Now all I have to do is carry out a daring rescue. But I am still scared, in truth, this time even more so.

The bay is full of tall ships, their masts and ropes and rolled-up sails clanking gently in the breeze. There is no sign of the rowboat or the pyrates from the *Curby Dodger*.

A ship is docked near the slave market. It sits low in the water and flies a Union Jack. While all the lights on deck are burning, the portholes are black. It's the slave ship. The sale is next morning at nine, according to a notice pinned up on the quay.

As I am reading, I feel a presence behind me. I spin round, ready to strike out or defend myself. But the figure is familiar.

'Toombi, thank goodness,' I gasp.

His face is serious; his eyes blink rapidly as he stares at the ship.

'We'll help them if we can,' I tell him. 'But first we have to save the captain and Billy and Catherine.' He listens intently as I tell him what happened, how they were captured in the Blue Mountains and taken to Fort George in Port Royal. 'They are to be hung in the morning,' I whisper. 'Where are the crew?'

The men are in a tavern, Toombi signs, spending their gold coins, drunk as skunks. From somewhere behind me comes the roaring of laughter and a short burst of the kind of seafaring song rarely sung by respectable seamen.

'And the rowboat?'

He points to the furthermost quay and indicates it is hidden.

'What shall we do?' I ask. Toombi glances across the water towards Gallows Point. He shrugs. How can a cabin boy, an escaped black slave and a dozen drunken pyrates take on every soldier in Port Royal and Kingston?

The rowboat will be somewhere to sleep at least. But as we walk along the jetty, I hear the sound of a child softly sobbing. I've heard that sob before.

'James,' I whisper. 'Is that you?'

The crying stops.

'Silas?'

I scan the jetty. A couple of other rowboats bob in the water, but it is too dark to see anything clearly

'I can't see you,' I whisper. 'Are you alone?'

'No,' he whispers back. 'But he's asleep.'

Toombi, who has heard everything, beckons me to follow him. There are two figures in the third boat along, one large and clearly out for the count, the other small and very much awake.

With one heave, Toombi shoves the sleeping man up and over the side of the boat. Just before he rolls, however, the man reaches out and grabs something. A chain uncoils at our feet. Before we can grab him, James is pulled over the side, yanked by the shackles that encircle his wrists.

When the man resurfaces, Toombi grabs an oar and bashes him on the head. In return, he grabs the oar and tries to pull Toombi in. As all this is happening, I scan the surface for James and see a single hand rise above the waves, grasp the air and then disappear.

Although I can't swim, I dive down into the water and flail wildly about in the watery blackness until finally my hand swipes the end of a chain. I take it in both hands and kick with all my strength until I reach the surface. I expect the worst, but it is Toombi who pulls me into the boat. James's guard is nowhere to be seen, so we haul in the chain, hand over fist, until finally James is beside the boat.

'Got you,' I say as we drag him back in. 'This is becoming a habit.'

I hear the whistle of a bullet just behind my head. I glance back and there, standing on the jetty, a pistol in his hand, is another of McGregor's men.

'Row!' I yell to Toombi. 'As fast as you can. To Port Royal!'

A bullet hits the bow and blasts a hole in the wood as big as my hand; fortunately it is above the water line.

In the bow, James coughs and splutters. He must have drunk a fair amount of seawater. Finally he lies back with his eyes open.

'The stars,' he says. 'Thought I was going to die without a final sight of them.'

'You're not going to die,' I tell him. 'At least, not yet.'

'He said he was going to kill me,' he gasps. 'Said my

mother had tricked him. If she didn't agree to marry him then he would kill us both.'

I don't need to ask him who he's talking about. McGregor is back in Jamaica.

# THE RUINED
# TOWN

In what seems like no time, Port Royal looms up in front of us. The old harbour, called Chocolata Hole, its steps crumbling and its moorings collapsing, is deathly silent. Fort George looms behind.

I know that the grizzled old pyrates and the drunken buccaneers, the lusty cut-throats and the murdering thieves who once lived on the spit of land called Port Royal, are long gone. Today, there is no other place in the Colonies that pyrates would do more to avoid. It is not just the Royal Navy Headquarters at Fort George, but the outcrop of land where the gallows are always built, a new one for each hanging. Just in case anyone should forget, there is a tiny islet called Deadman's Cay on the far side of the

Fort, where the dead body of Calico Jack, the famous pyrate, was tarred and hung in a cage as a warning to others.

No wonder Port Royal has become a place of bad ends and nightmares, of ghosts and untimely demises.

We row as quietly as we can along the edge of the half-sunken city left behind by the earthquake and tidal wave so long ago. The remains of the town rise out of the water, its crumbling walls towering above us like cliffs. Half in the water, half out, a carriage with a wheel missing and its upholstery covered in seaweed sits in what might have been the entrance to a stable.

A vast doorway, one side half-toppled, the other leaning so far to the right it looks about to collapse, has a faded painted sign that reads *The Sugar Loaf*. Inside, it is pitch black. Who knows what is there? Toombi lifts an oar, causing us to veer sharply to the right and head silently through the door of the sunken tavern.

Here we spend a sleepless night. I assure James that although it wasn't easy, we did deliver the jewels to Dunlop.

'But then McGregor burst in and stole them.' I tell him more, whispering in the darkness.

'So they were only made of glass!' James is shocked and, for a moment, silent. The jewels, it seems, have not brought him and his mother good fortune.

'But Dunlop knew them,' I tell James. 'He's your father! And he is coming.' I pull the handkerchief from my pocket. 'And he gave me this to hand to your mother in return.'

In the light of the moon, James stares at the two initials:

$$\mathcal{I} \ \& \ \mathcal{A}$$

'I thought his name was William?'

I decide that this is not the time or the place to reveal to James his father's true identity.

'Your mother will know it,' I say. 'It is her own needlework.'

He frowns then hands it back.

'But what good will it do now?' he says. 'McGregor has taken her.'

'Taken her where?'

'To the ship, to your old ship.'

'To the *Tenacity*? Where is she moored?'

James shakes his head.

'I don't know. But I do know that if he doesn't get what he wants, he has sworn to set the ship alight and let it go down with all hands.'

James blinks back a tear.

'Even hers,' he says.

They say it is always darkest just before the dawn. And it is just before sunrise that we hear the sound of hammering in the distance.

'What's that?' James asks.

'They've started to build the gallows.'

# THE HANGING

We climb up a set of crumbling steps and from the vantage point of an attic room in the old tavern we can see everything. Gallows Point sticks out into the bay just beyond Fort George. Dozens of ships have left their moorings in Kingston and dropped anchor off the point to watch the hangings. Wealthy plantation owners and their wives, dressed up in their Sunday best, sit under the shade of colourful parasols on the decks of chartered boats. The rest, shop owners and harbour masters, bookkeepers and tavern boys, bob up and down in hired rowing boats. In fact, it seems as if the entire population of the town has turned out.

The gallows, newly built and still splintery and sticky with sap, sits on a bluff of grass above a small sandy bay. The ocean rolls lazily back and forth on the shore while the wind sighs softly along the beach. I wish for tornados or rainstorms, earthquakes or tidal waves but, judging by the sky, it is going to be a beautiful day. As the sun lights up the rope that hangs in three loops from the crossbeam of the gallows, I am filled with a cold, reckless misery. To be so close and to be able to do nothing is the worst feeling in the world.

With a creak, the metal door of the fort opens. A drum starts to beat as a doctor comes out, followed by a man dressed in black. The crowd bursts into a round of applause. I can't bear it any longer. Without telling James or Toombi, I slip away, and creep down the stairs. I wade out of the tavern's front door and through a large archway that was once the town's main gate. And then I crouch behind a pile of rubble, the ruins of the town wall. I can see the man in black, the executioner, checking the gallows over, testing the ropes and the trapdoors beneath. The point is so exposed that I cannot get anywhere near without being spotted.

I edge around the back and approach the fort from behind, from the beach. The walls are steep and higher than they look, but I am good at climbing and within a few minutes, am up and over the top. As quietly as I can, I drop down on to the yellow dust of the parade ground.

The prison is right in the middle of the fort. It has a door at the front and three barred windows at the back. The door is guarded, so I make a run for the back. Nobody spots me, no one is looking. Once I get my breath back, I climb up until I can see through one of the windows. Directly on the floor below, sitting in a shaft of sunlight, is the captain.

'Captain! Up here,' I whisper. 'It's Silas!'

Black Johnnie turns and squints into the light.

'Silas?' he repeats. When he sees that it is, in fact, me, his cabin boy, he doesn't look very pleased.

'You must leave immediately. What on earth do you think you're doing?

'Toombi is with me,' I go on. 'Don't lose heart. We're trying to find a way.'

But he doesn't seem to hear me.

'Promise me something. Get out of here immediately. That is an order.'

I hesitate, I hum, I haw.

'Promise me!' he repeats. 'It is my last wish.'

What can I do but promise?

Just then the door swings open and a great, ugly guard comes in. I duck down. He farts loudly before he speaks.

'On your feet. You've been entertained here for far too long. The time has come, you grubby vagabond, the time has come to take a drop, to go for a sail, to meet your maker.'

And then he laughs, as if he has said something amusing, which he certainly hasn't.

I slide down the prison wall until I am sitting at the bottom. What now? We are two boys and a former slave against the British Navy. We can't fight them alone. We have no weapons, no plan, nothing.

The drum has started to beat again and the crowds on the boats let out a huge cheer. 'Swing them,' a voice booms out. 'Swing them high!' shouts another. 'Let's see the pyrates hang!' yells a third.

Only a miracle can save them now.

I sit so still that a lizard shoots out of a crack in the brickwork and starts when it sees me. And then, with a flick of its tail, it darts back again. I wish that I could follow it. I wish that I could crawl into a hole and die. Instead, I know I must make myself stand up and try and get back out of the fort. I promised the captain.

I edge out of the shade and make a run for the nearest section of wall. From here, I slip around the perimeter, but, to my horror, run headlong into a soldier coming the other way.

But instead of grabbing me or raising the alarm, he simply gives me a strange look and keeps on running towards the entrance of the fort.

With my heart pounding, I scale the wall, clamber up and over the other side, and make a run for the edge of the ruined town. Once more I can lie flat out on the grass without being seen. The captain, Billy the Fiddle and Catherine are standing in a row to the right of the gallows. Each has a black hood over their head. But the drummer has stopped drumming. A plume of smoke rises above Kingston. The church bell is ringing. Something is happening.

Since voices carry much further on water than on land, even though they are quite far away, I can hear the plantation owners shouting to each other from boat to boat.

'The slaves...' one shouts. 'They are escaping!'

'But I have just paid handsomely,' says another. 'I can't afford to lose that money.'

'Pull up the anchor,' shouts a third. 'We must return immediately!'

'Who could have done such a thing?' wails a woman. 'They cannot have released themselves!'

I have an idea who might have crept into the empty town looking for me, found the slaves in their pen and freed them: Oscar, Jonathan and the others. I shake my fist in the air with joy. Good work!

As the flotilla of boats off Gallows Point pull up their anchors, turn around and head back to town, two dozen soldiers from the Fort climb aboard a dinghy and follow them. Only three are left behind, along with the doctor and the executioner. Maybe they will call off the hanging? But one by one the executioner pushes the prisoners up the gallows steps until the captain, Billy the Fiddle and Catherine each stand in front of a noose.

I remember the advice Black Johnnie once gave me. When in doubt, do the opposite of what they would expect. The soldiers have a musket each, but I know that now is the time. It is now or never.

I look around for something to arm myself with but find nothing. I have only my slingshot. I pull it out of my pocket and place a pebble in its cradle. Then I stand up, hold it out in front of me, let out a blood-curdling cry and charge.

'Yaaaaaarrrrr!'

As I run across the grass towards the gallows, the expression on the faces of the soldiers slowly changes. It starts with surprise and then transforms into fear. The sight of me must be more frightening than I ever expected. But even before I reach them I am aware of the dull rumble of footsteps behind me. I glance over my shoulder. And there, led by Toombi, armed with axes and swords, machetes and cutlasses, their faces scarred or covered in tattoos, is the crew of the *Curby*

*Dodger*. Toombi must have gone back to fetch them. No wonder the soldiers drop their weapons and hold up their hands.

'Get to your knees,' shouts one pyrate, who has clearly done this sort of thing before. 'One move and you'll get my knife through your heart.'

The soldiers offer no resistance. The doctor starts to sob and his knees give way of their own accord. Only the executioner jumps off the gallows and tries to make a run for it. The pyrates catch up with him on the beach.

'This is for my brother,' says one and gives him a punch in the belly. 'You strung him up three years ago.'

'And this is for my father,' says another, giving him a kick. 'When he swung, he left ten children to starve.'

'No doubt he deserved it,' the executioner yelled.

The pyrates, as one, all raise their weapons. The executioner cowers with his hands above his head.

'Stop,' yells the captain. Toombi has pulled the black hoods from their heads. The three condemned prisoners stand blinking in the bright sunlight. 'Don't hurt him.'

The pyrates are astonished – speechless in fact.

'Don't hurt him, after all he's done?'

'But that's not right. We need vengeance!'

'Then row him out to Deadman's Cay and leave him

there,' says Black Johnnie. 'Let him take his chances with the tide. A slow death is far, far worse than a swift one.'

This, the pyrates all agree, is true.

Across the bay, Kingston harbour is filled with boats all jostling with each other to dock. Even from here we can tell by the raised voices and the clash of bow on bow that there is pandemonium. The town, in contrast, has gone deadly quiet. I hope the slaves have run as fast as they can in all directions. I hope they never get caught.

Black Johnnie, Billy the Fiddle and Catherine are helped off the gallows. Someone produces a bottle of rum and they all, even Catherine, take a drink.

'Well, that was a near thing,' says Billy and rubs his neck.

'You broke your promise,' the captain says sternly to me.

My face grows hot and then cold again.

'I had no choice,' I reply.

And then he hugs me so hard that I think I might suffocate.

'I forgive you this time,' he whispers. 'Will somebody please tell me? Where have all the people gone?'

'I think the children did it,' I say. 'Catherine's friends. I met them after you were captured. They freed the slaves in Kingston. They saved us all.'

Catherine face breaks into the sweetest smile but she says nothing.

Then it all seems to dawn on us at the same time. The three prisoners have escaped the gallows but how can we all now escape Port Royal?

'If only we had the *Tenacity*,' says Billy the Fiddle.

And then sailing round the headland, almost as if she had heard us, comes our ship.

# TWO SHIPS

It feels as if it takes an hour for the *Tenacity* to reach us, but in truth it cannot have been more than a few minutes. The beautiful ship sails right into the harbour and drops anchor. As we watch, a woman in a white dress appears on the deck.

'Who on earth?' says Black Johnnie.

'It's Isabella,' I say.

Behind her are three of McGregor's men, all armed with muskets. And then a thought occurs to me.

'Where's James?' I ask.

No one has seen him for quite some time. I'm starting to get a bad feeling. And then a voice shouts out.

'Mama?'

McGregor and James are standing on the crumbling steps at Chocolata Hole. He has a knife to the boy's throat.

'I will kill the boy,' he shouts to us. 'Unless you agree to my demands.'

'James,' Isabella cries out. 'Please! He is my son. Don't hurt him.'

'Send a skiff for us both,' he shouts to his men. 'And then send it back for the prisoners, the black man and that boy.'

My joy turns to despair in an instant. Whatever he wants us for cannot be good. Black Johnnie rubs his neck as if he can feel the noose around it again. Even Billy the Fiddle cannot even think of anything cheerful to say. To almost die once in one day is bad enough.

'Go,' the captain tells the pyrates who remain. 'Go back into Port Royal. The soldiers won't find you there.'

But they do not move. They stand in silence as the skiff returns and, one by one, we climb inside.

'We'll be here,' one says. 'If you need us.'

'Thank you,' says Black Johnnie.

By the time the captain, Billy the Fiddle, Catherine, Toombi and I reach the decks of the *Tenacity*, James is being comforted by Isabella. Her face is dirty and the dress is torn. She can't have come aboard without a struggle. McGregor, however, has changed into a fresh waistcoat and jacket.

'Well, well,' he says. 'You are as slippery as eels, it seems I need to keep my enemies close.'

He casts a glance back at Kingston. Now the commotion has died down a little, a few boats have begun to head back in the direction of Port Royal to see what has transpired.

'Pull up the anchors,' McGregor shouts. 'We need a little privacy, I think.'

As I have said, with the wind blowing in the right direction, the *Tenacity* can move at quite a clip. Today, the surface of the sea is tipped with white and the westerly breeze is filled with dashes of rain. In no time, the island of Jamaica is just a blue rock on the horizon.

'What is he going to do to us?' I ask the captain.

Black Johnnie shakes his head.

'I have no idea,' he says.

'Isabella,' McGregor says. 'It is time. Captain Harkin. Please?'

And then I get it.

'He wants you to marry him!' I say.

The captain shudders.

'I cannot marry him,' he says. 'He is a man!'

'Not *you*: Isabella! He wants you to marry him and Isabella!'

'But I have no authority...' he begins.

'Catherine?' I say. 'Tell him.'

'A ship's captain can record births and deaths,' she says. 'And he can marry people, I think.'

So it is that the captain stands on the bridge with Isabella and McGregor in front of him and two of McGregor's men pointing their muskets behind.

'Captain McGregor,' says Isabella, 'I beg you to reconsider.'

'The jewels were glass and the reward a piffling amount,' he says. 'This seems a far better prize for all my effort. I lost my ship, you know.'

'I didn't mean...' Isabella begins.

'Enough,' he says. 'Your father isn't young anymore. You are his only heir. This way, I will be the next Duke of Rothesay, and his fortune and yours will be mine. And our children's, of course.'

Isabella shivers.

'If I do this, will you promise James can stay with me?' she asks.

'Why should I?' McGregor replies. 'The world is a cruel place, is it not, Jon Harkin?'

Isabella begins to weep. I am standing near enough to pass her the red handkerchief I still carry. She takes it gratefully, wipes her eyes, then looks harder at it. She steals a glance straight at me, and I give the smallest nod. She looks as though she does not know whether to be full of joy or full of sorrow. It is a sign that all is well, but it has come too late.

'Begin,' insists McGregor. His men point their muskets at each of us.

'We are gathered here together...' Black Johnnie pauses. His eye is drawn to something just behind Isabella's head.

'Would there be any chance of asking your men to stand in front? It puts me off, them being behind.'

McGregor sighs.

'Men,' he shouts. 'Position yourself behind me. But keep your aim. Is this your final wish, Harkin?'

'No,' he replies. 'Could you, the groom, take off your armaments for the ceremony – your sword, musket and the like. They make me nervous.'

With a shake of his head, McGregor takes off his holster, his sword and his scabbard and lays them on the ground next to the mast.

'What else would you like?' he says. 'A glass of rum to settle your stomach. A cigar? I'm joking, obviously.'

He smiles a grotesque grin, revealing that his teeth are black and rotten. Black Johnnie gives him a weak smile in return.

'Now get on with it,' McGregor says.

'As you know,' the captain says, 'holy matrimony is

not something that should be entered into lightly. It is a legal bond that commits a man and woman together until death does them part.'

He pauses for a moment.

'The laws of the land are such that none should be taken asunder... in sickness as well as in health...'

Billy the Fiddle catches my eye. The captain is stalling for time. I take a quick peak over my shoulder. A ship is approaching.

'To have and to hold,' the captain says. 'To hold all... I'm particularly fond of holdalls. They can carry much and yet do not take up much space.'

McGregor suddenly lunges at Black Johnnie and grabs him by the collar.

'It's a metaphor,' the captain says. 'About the human heart. Nothing more.'

McGregor runs a sharpened fingernail across the captain's cheek. Then lets him go.

'We do not want blood on my wife's dress, do we?' he says. 'So get on with it.'

The captain brushes down his clothes and starts again.

'As a ship's captain,' he says. 'By the authority vested in God and the State.'

And here he takes a deep breath and holds out his hand to Isabella.

'Did we meet before?' he asks. 'I think not.'

He shakes her hand.

'I am getting,' McGregor says loudly, 'impatient!'

'It's customary,' says the captain, 'to meet the betrothed before she becomes a bride, is it not?'

I can hear the creak of the ropes and the wash of sea against wood. The ship is coming closer. It could be a slave ship or a merchant vessel, a naval schooner or a pyrate ship. Is it friend or foe? Black Johnnie's hands are beginning to shake. He speaks a little louder.

'Anyway, where were we? I had met the bride and was considering the idea of holding all...'

'Right!' yells McGregor. 'For every minute you delay, one of your party shall be thrown overboard, starting with the girl.'

'As I was saying,' says Black Johnnie. 'Marriage. I'll skip all the usual bits. Let's see now. Do you... Albert – Is that your name? Unfortunate – Albert McGregor... Any middle names? ... No, don't tell me – we are in a rush – take this lady... My good lady, do you have a second name? Never mind – Do you, Albert, take you, Isabella, to be your lawfully wedded wife?'

'I do,' says McGregor.

'And you, Isabella...'

Once more I see his eyes flick over her shoulder. In turn, she glances round. I dare not look, I dare not.

'Do you take this man...?'

There is a thump behind as two feet land on the deck. She blinks, she smiles. And then she shakes her head.

'Never!' she declares firmly.

We all swing round. There before us, his sword drawn, stands William Dunlop. His ship, a small schooner that flies a Blue Jolly Roger, has pulled up alongside us without McGregor or his men noticing. He's good. No wonder he was such a successful pyrate.

# WALKING THE PLANK

'McGregor?' he says. 'What's going on?'

'Mr Dunlop!' replies McGregor, his face white with astonishment.

Dunlop looks different from when we met him in Glasgow. His face is brown and he wears his hair long down his neck.

'So?' the shipbuilding millionaire says. 'What cargo do you transport today? Women?'

McGregor turns and looks for his men. All are being held at knifepoint by Dunlop's seamen.

'Have you come looking for your jewels?' McGregor asks. 'Those I found at your house were worth nothing! The jeweller I took them to laughed in my face. I threw them into the Clyde.'

'But now it seems I have found my jewel,' Dunlop says softly.

He looks across at Isabella and smiles. Only a fool would not be struck by how happy they are to see each other. Isabella blushes, and then her face suddenly changes.

'Avery!' she yells. 'Look out.'

From out of nowhere comes the Chinese girl, the one McGregor hired who made me jump overboard that night in Martinique. The former pyrate ducks as a knife whistles over his head.

'Avery!' says McGregor. 'Not Avery Blue, the pyrate?'

'The same,' replies Dunlop as he turns his attention to the girl. She leaps towards him. He leaps towards her. For one moment they are a tumble of arms and legs, steel and rope. And then he stands back. She sits, disarmed and tied up.

'Learned that little trick in Shanghai,' Dunlop says.

While all this has been happening, McGregor has been heading, almost casually towards his weapons. Dunlop, however, is too quick. With one foot, he kicks the musket over the side.

'Your actions, McGregor, are indefensible,' he says. 'Kidnap, forced marriage, theft, abuse, assault.'

The boat hits a swell and begins to tip. The wind

is rising. The sword slides across the deck and reaches McGregor before Dunlop can stop it.

'You're Avery Blue,' he says picking up the sword. 'My crimes are nothing compared to yours.'

'He's dead. I am William Dunlop.'

'Why do this?' McGregor asks. 'You, a wealthy man? You have so much to lose.'

'I've come to claim something which means more to me than my wealth,' says Dunlop.

'What would that be?' McGregor replies. 'This ship and everything on it is mine.

'Actually,' Black Johnnie points out, 'this ship is *mine*.'

'You lose either way,' McGregor tells Dunlop. 'Either you die by my sword or you will swing like your friends here. Unless, that is, you'd like to strike another bargain? The lady's life in exchange for your fortune.'

'I don't make bargains with swindlers,' Dunlop says.

Dunlop and McGregor begin to fight, sword clashing against sword. It is soon clear, however, that Dunlop has the advantage. Sensing this, McGregor lunges for Isabella. Once more he has her by the neck.

'Get off me!' she gasps.

'I will kill her in ten seconds if you do not do as I say.' Dunlop stands back.

'Don't hurt her,' he says.

'I will take your ship,' McGregor nods at Dunlop's

schooner. 'In return, I shall not unmask you, Avery Blue. At least not today.'

The ship is rocked by a huge wave. The sky is darkening in the west. A few drops of rain become a shower.

'Go then,' Dunlop says, motioning towards the gangplank that links the two vessels. With his arm around Isabella's neck, McGregor steps over the railings.

'But be careful,' says Dunlop.

'The boy comes with me,' McGregor demands.

'What!'

'How do I know you will not chase me?' he says. 'I will put him off in Kingston.'

'No!' says Isabella.

'I'll go,' James is trying to look brave.

'Good. You cross first!' demands McGregor.

Gingerly, James walks across the gangplank. Once he is on the other ship, McGregor, still holding Isabella, takes a step.

'Let her go now,' the captain says.

'Not yet,' McGregor says, 'not until I'm halfway across.'

He does not see the huge wave that breaks on the bow, causing the gangplank to lurch suddenly. Instead, he loses his footing and is thrown backwards. Isabella falls forward, twists in the air and at the last moment catches hold of the plank with her fingertips.

'Mama!' James yells.

'Isabella!' yells Dunlop.

The sea boils beneath her as she swings back and forth. The waves keep coming, hitting the bows of both ships with increasing force. McGregor regains his balance and stands up on the plank.

'I cannot hold on for much longer,' Isabella screams.

'Save her,' yells Black Johnnie.

McGregor turns and looks back at us, his eyes filled with ice-cold fury.

'Save her yourself,' he says.

He takes one step and then another, slowly crossing the plank. When he comes to the place where Isabella hangs, he laughs. And then, to our horror, he places one boot and then the next on Isabella's fingers.

The shot rings out before any of us can react. McGregor flies backwards clutching his chest and falls into the rolling waves below. Toombi stands on the bow of the *Tenacity* with a musket in his hand.

I stare down at the sea. Nothing breaks its surface.

Isabella still hangs between the ships.

The swell has risen, the rain is driving, and, with a creak, the vessels push together. The gangplank lashed between them groans with the pressure and starts to split.

'No!' yells Isabella, as her left hand slips and lets go.

'I'm going to her,' shouts Dunlop.

'It will not take your weight,' I yell. 'Undo the gangplank.'

'What?' yells Dunlop.

'Quickly!' I yell. 'Before it breaks in two! Then push it over!'

Billy the Fiddle brings out a knife and slices through the ropes. The schooner is almost right below us now. The end of the gangplank, suddenly unleashed from the ropes that have secured it, shoots up in the air. We push until it rises up and over, until Isabella and the plank fall with a clatter on to the schooner's deck. James rushes to her. He turns and waves: she's safe. We all let out a sigh of relief.

'Who was left on board?' Dunlop demands. 'Which seamen are there?'

One of his men shakes his head.

'You told us all to come with you,' another says. 'There's no one else on board.'

And then it dawns on him.

'They're alone! How will they sail?' Dunlop cries out.

# THE RAINBOW

We watch, helpless, as Dunlop's vessel, tossed by the wind and carried by the swell, is born away. Dunlop climbs onto the railings and prepares to jump but it is too far.

'You'll never make it,' says Black Johnnie.

'Then what?' he shouts. 'Do something!'

Immediately, Black Johnnie takes command. He knows the *Tenacity*, her speed, her bulk, her ways.

'Raise the mainstay,' he shouts. 'We go after her.'

The storm has reached its height and the sea rises up and down, its surface white with spray and slashed with rain. Out in front, the schooner's sails rip and tear and she is tossed back and forth. Our fear is that she will capsize, until we see a greater danger.

'The reefs!' I yell.

I turn and look at Black Johnnie. He knows. His mouth is a line, his eyes narrow.

'Go faster!' yells Dunlop.

Finally we reach the stricken schooner, but we cannot get too close for fear of ramming her. Instead we sail beside her.

'Put out our plank!' Dunlop shouts.

'It will not reach!' Billy the Fiddle yells back.

'Move closer!' Dunlop shouts.

'I cannot!' screams the captain.

And then I know what I must do. As quick as I can, I climb the rigging until I'm at the top of the mast.

'Get down,' yells Dunlop. 'What is the boy doing?'

But the captain and Billy the Fiddle already know.

'Knots!' shouts Bill. 'Tie them well.'

'Get ready to duck,' Black Johnnie says. 'I'll get as close as I can, Silas.'

The reefs are a dark bloom beneath the water. The schooner is almost upon them.

Once I am tied and tied again, I wait until I cannot wait any longer. And then I hold on tight, lean over and push myself off the mast. I fall, down, down until I can taste the sea in my mouth and feel its spray on my face. And then, just as I'm about to hit its surface, I start to swing back, back across the decks, past all the seaman, and over the other side until the sea is below me again. For a moment I close my eyes and when I open them I'm high, high above the schooner. I take a deep breath. And then I let go.

It would be fair to say that my landing is not the most elegant. I roll over and over and end up sprawled beside the privy.

'Are you all right?' asks Isabella.

I nod my head.

'I think so,' I say.

And then from down below comes the awful sound of coral on wood. We've hit the reef. The *Tenacity* has dropped her sails. She cannot follow us now. I hear a voice carried from far away by the wind.

'Take the wheel,' yells Black Johnnie. 'Steer her well.'

I run to the bridge and push a wooden box to the wheel. Once I stand on it, I can see over. We have hit *El Cascabel*, the tail of *La Vibora*, the viper, the treacherous bank of reef and sand and rock.

'Look!' says Isabella. To our right are the smashed up remains of three ships.

'Go below!' I shout to James. 'See how bad it is.'

He runs back a moment later.

'We're letting in a little water.' he says. 'Shall I bail?'

I shake my head, no.

'Help me,' I say. 'One go to port, the other starboard. Tell me what you see?'

But the wind blows so strong, the surface of the sea is opaque.

We hit another submerged reef and, once again, we can hear the coral scrape and rip at our bow. This sounds even worse than the first. Water begins to rush into the hull.

'You tried,' calls Isabella. 'And for that we thank you from the bottom of our hearts.'

I have not given up yet. I remember following the dolphin as we sailed through the narrow channel many months ago. I remember the noise and the crash of cannonballs as they ripped through the sails. I remember reaching the other side.

'We'll get through this!' I shout. 'I promise!'

With both hands on the wheel, I veer left, I veer right, I act on a hunch, on a whim, on the colour of air. Twice, I turn too hard and we almost capsize.

'Not so hard,' yells James as the whole boat tips.

But I can see what he can't. We have just missed another wreck, most of it underwater with only its main mast to show what deadly fate lies beneath.

We're almost there; I can see the deep blue of the shipping channel just ahead. But suddenly, right in front of us, is the pale green of a submerged sandbank.

'Unfurl the mainstay!' I yell. 'We need speed. We're going over.'

'What?' shouts James. 'Are you sure?'

'Trust me.'

But in truth, I do not trust myself. I can feel the *Tenacity*'s crew watching us from afar. I can sense their dismay, their hands thrown over their mouths and eyes. It looks, I know, like I am going to sink the ship. It looks as if I have lost my mind.

'Hold on!' I shout as the wind rises behind us.

Later, I will tell people that it was the current, or the shallow draft, or the right kind of wind in our sails. But at that moment it feels as if Avery Blue's vessel has decided she can fly, because we lift up and skim over the sandbank, almost without a ripple on our wake.

'We've done it!' Isabella says. 'You clever, clever boy!'

'We're safe now,' I say.

I try to remove my hands from wheel to wipe the sweat and rain from my brow, but I have been holding on so tightly, they are almost stuck fast.

'Look,' shouts James.

What now, I think, more rocks? But he is pointing at the sky. The rain has almost stopped, the sun has come out, and a huge rainbow arches above the distant island of Jamaica.

'Silas,' a voice calls out from far away. 'Are you all right?'

'No,' I say, 'I don't think I am.'

My last thought before I lose consciousness is of handfuls of coloured glass jewels catching the light as they sink slowly downwards through the watery depths of the river Clyde.

# SWEET
# PARTINGS

'This will wake him up,' says a child's voice I recognise but can't place.

The shock of a bucket of ice-cold water in the face is so much that for a moment I cannot open my eyes.

'What was that for?' I yell.

Another child starts to snigger. I open my eyes. Jonathan and the children are standing all around me.

'He's not dead,' says Oscar.

'Of course I'm not dead,' I reply. 'Where did you come from?'

'We swam out. It wasn't far.'

I sit up. Somehow I have ended up on the *Tenacity* again. We are anchored in a beautiful bay. I look up and see a large house on a hill. On the beach, more children are playing. One of them, I can see from here, is James.

'Where are we?' I ask.

'James's house,' Oscar replies.

I wonder, for a moment, if I am still dreaming. The sea is as clear as glass and the large garden that stretches all the way to the beach is full of flowers.

'Isn't it beautiful?' a girl's voice says.

Catherine is standing on the railings. She jumps down and smiles.

'Have you steered many ships?' she asks.

'Not many,' I reply.

'That was quite something...'

'I'd like never to repeat.'

She laughs.

'Where is the schooner?' I ask.

'It sank,' she says simply as if it were the only thing it could possibly do. 'But you'd got it through the reefs, which meant we could get close to you. James threw down the anchor and we got you all aboard the *Tenacity*.'

Jonathan cocks his head to one side. He's heard something: the hoot of a signal calling them back. Catherine's heard it as well.

'We need to go,' he says.

'You, too?' I ask.

She nods her head then stares out at the ocean.

'But one day we'll probably join you on the high seas,' she says. 'So watch your back.'

For another week, we pyrates lie low at the plantation. Dunlop and Isabella, parted for years, make plans. With a family to look after and a plantation to run, Dunlop decides to sell his shipbuilding business in Glasgow and move to Jamaica.

'But a life at sea still beckons me,' he tells Black Johnnie when Isabella is out of the room. 'And I have heard of prizes that will make your hair stand on end.'

The reward Dunlop gives to each of us for reuniting him with Isabella and James is secret. Nobody knows what anyone else received. He gave me a bag of twenty gold coins, all for myself, easily enough to establish myself, should I wish to leave the pyrating life.

Once the *Tenacity* has been re-stocked with supplies, the hull painted with pitch and the sails and rigging repaired, she prepares to sail. The captain has a full crew made up of any pyrate who wanted to join us and will swear loyalty. Some come from the *Curby Dodger* and others from the old *Tenacity* crew, who had made their way to Jamaica from the Windward Isles.

I lie down in my berth. It's been a long time but nothing much has changed. I see a loose board and lift it. There is nothing there. A noise makes me look to the doorway. Toombi is there, watching me, smiling. He holds up the key to the lead box.

'But where is my old stash now?' asks Black Johnnie when I rush up on deck to tell him.

Toombi fetches parchment and ink and the captain's quill pen, and sketches us a map of the island where we found him after the volcano explosion in Martinique. He draws the stream then carefully indicates the trees and the stones. On one of the stones he marks a large

'You stole my stash from McGregor?' the captain asks. 'Using the key that Silas hid?'

Toombi's smile is wider than the sun. He nods. And then he signs that it still belongs to Black Johnnie.

'Good man,' the captain says. 'Well, it seems that that I now have a new proposition. We find the island and I will share out my old rough diamonds.'

The pyrates' eyes grow glassy. They can almost feel the weight of the rocks in their hands.

'You – *you* – mislaid a fortune in diamonds?' Bill asks, half-amused.

'Someone swapped them for a few handfuls of glass,'

says the captain. 'But what of this new proposal, what do you say?'

As one they all say, 'Aye!'

For a moment, I hesitate. My sister has a life in Scotland now; she is established. And I have enough money to set myself up in Jamaica as I once wished: to buy a small plantation perhaps, near Dunlop, Isabella and James. But what of my life on the ocean? What of adventure and danger and treasure?

'I like a shiny shoe and a clean shirt,' the captain says softly.

'You need a boy?' I ask

'Only if his name is Silas,' he replies. 'What do you say?'

'Yes!' I say. 'Ten, twenty, thirty times: yes.'

'Bring to,' Billy the Fiddle shouts from the bridge. 'Keep her full before the wind! Aloft!'

I look back at the island of Jamaica, at the Blue Mountains and the dark green jungle, as streaks of ruby and silver and gold fill the darkening sky like the promise of things to come.

# THE END

# WAR. FRIENDSHIP. FOOTBALL.

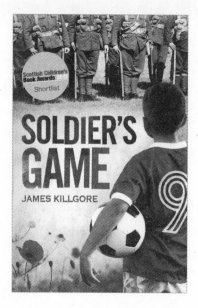

Ross loves football, but his team won't stop losing! After another humiliating defeat, Ross is given an old pair of football boots, which once belonged to his grand-father, Jack Jordan. Ross can't believe that no one ever told him Jack played for his favourite team, the famous Heart of Midlothian FC.

As Ross finds out more about Jack, an incredible story unfolds – a tale of Edinburgh's young heroes and a battalion of footballers and fans who fought in the First World War.

This book is based on the remarkable true story of the 16th Royal Scots, known as the "Hearts Battalion".

Also available as an eBook.

**discoverkelpies.co.uk**

# A deadly virus. Fierce pirates. Hungry Dogs.
# Who will win this race for survival?

The deadly red fever virus has killed most of the people on Earth and Scotland is a wasteland overrun by wild dogs. Can Toby save his family from the danger surrounding them?

Also available as an eBook.

**discoverkelpies.co.uk**

# Secrets, Adventure
## Laughter AND DANGER...

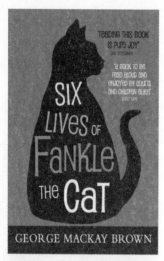

SIX LIVES OF FANKLE THE CAT

"reading this book is pure joy"
THE SCOTSMAN

"a book to be read aloud and enjoyed by adults and children alike"
SUNDAY TIMES

GEORGE MACKAY BROWN

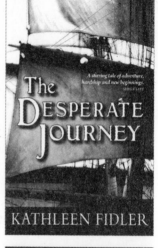

The DESPERATE JOURNEY

A stirring tale of adventure, hardship and new beginnings.
SHELF LIFE

KATHLEEN FIDLER

A STRANGER CAME ASHORE

MOLLIE HUNTER

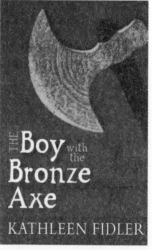

THE Boy with the Bronze Axe

KATHLEEN FIDLER

## WITH THE KELPIES CLASSICS